S0-EAQ-853

Always Connected

Always Connected

Genevieve Galvan Frenes

Always Connected

Copyright © 2015 Genevieve Galvan Frenes

All rights reserved. No part of this publication may be reproduced, stored in a retrieval system or transmitted in any form or by any means, electronic, mechanical, photocopying, recording or otherwise, without the prior written permission of the copyright holder, except for brief quotations used in a review.

This is a work of fiction. Names, characters, places, and incidents are the product of the author's imagination or are used fictitiously, and any resemblance to any actual persons, living or dead, events, or locales is entirely coincidental.

Paperback
    ISBN-13: 978-1517539634
    ISBN-10: 1517539633

Ebook
    ASIN: B015UL6RKA

Cover design by: Kayla Montemayor
Cover layout by: Melissa Summers
Edited by: Lorna Collins

Always Connected is a powerful tale about loss, acceptance, and the power of faith. This compelling novel about a family thrown into chaos is pregnant with hope and guidance for those who have suffered the loss of a loved one. Inspirational, uplifting, and highly recommended.

~ John M. Wills, award-winning author of ***Healer***, ***The Year Without Christmas*** and other fine books ~

A long-forgotten love affair comes back to haunt Nicholas when he receives an email from a grown daughter he didn't know existed. A poignant story told from his point of view and those of his wife and children. The author is a wonderful storyteller and does a terrific job of portraying all the family members' emotions.

~ Cheryl Gardarian, author of ***The Cookie Tree***, ***The Unexpected Reunion***, ***The Cabin***, and co-author of the Aspen Grove romance anthology series ~

Courage, fear, anxiety, and love are those emotions wrapped up in this engaging novel of a young woman who recently discovers an aspect of her life, which she has known nothing about. The author has skillfully created a cast of characters who come to make a difference in broadening Sarah's world. For anyone who has been affected by adoption, ***Always Connected*** is a charming story that relates both heartbreak and heartfelt gratitude in developing relationships with a new family.

~ Pauline Crawford Crabb, Phd, retired educator, artist, and author of ***My Life Defined*** ~

For some people, human actions are only random events that sometimes coalesce into coincidences. For Genevieve Frenes, every human life is a thread that is woven into a spectacular tapestry by the hand of a Master Weaver. In this first novel, she testifies to the power of faith to heal past wounds and enable us to remain ***Always Connected***, not by accident but by design.

~ Fr. Daniel Avila, Director of Vocations, Diocese of Fresno ~

The author of **Always Connected** illustrates a journey on a road that many families travel. Her story opens the door to communication that is not only inspiring but therapeutic in understanding how life WILL happen and how Faith will allow healing to take residence in the heart of every household. Great read for individuals and families, which have experienced a loss, looking for a place to start.

~ Clara A Brown, Professional School Counselor ~

FOREWORD

This book was inspired by real events. However, any resemblance to actual people or circumstances is purely coincidental.

I share this story with others who have had similar experiences. I hope those affected by the loss of children, whose existence was kept hidden, will be encouraged to pursue relationships with them. This story is for those children and their families.

May blessings come to those who choose to love.

DEDICATION

This novel is dedicated to:

My Lord.
In all situations, in all joys and in
all sorrows, He has been present
in my life, has guided me in all
things, and has brought me to
this place.

My husband, David Molina
Frenes, Jr.
You are my companion and
friend for life and the most
blessed man I know. For all of
your encouragement and support
during this process, I love you
beyond words.

My children: Jacquelyn, Faith,
Marissa, Haley, and Isaiah David.
You are the greatest blessings of
my life.

ACKNOWLEDGMENTS

I would like to acknowledge many individuals who have supported and guided me in the process of writing my first novel.

First and foremost, I would like to thank Paula May, my mentor not only in teaching, but also in life. Your insight and grace are the foundations of a true teacher and leader in life. Thank you for always encouraging me in my writing and speaking with wisdom and humility. You have encouraged me to trust in my words and tell my story.

I would like to thank Gaynl Potter, my colleague and schoolmate. You were the first to know about our story, and you helped me to cope and deal with feelings I truly did not know how to handle. Thank you for always being the positive voice, which reassured me to believe in myself, despite my setbacks with the writing process.

A special thanks to Mrs. Darleen Johnson for her help on editing and reviewing the material in its initial stages. Your help was greatly appreciated.

Thank you to Lorna Collins, my copy editor and guide in the process of this novel. As my first experience in writing and publishing, you made me feel at ease from the start and helped make my dream of becoming an author come to life. I am so grateful to have found you.

I want to thank my parents, Michael and Margarite Galvan, immediate family and friends who encouraged me to write and gave me the strength not to give up when I began to doubt.

I especially want to thank my husband, David, who has allowed me to share this experience with the world. You are truly a man of God, and I am blessed to be married to my best friend. Your choice to accept, embrace, and love your child, even though you did not know about her until later in her life, only shows the world even more what I already knew existed in your heart. In my eyes, you are the greatest father our children could have, and the most loving man I will ever know.

I am grateful to my children for their grace in dealing with the surprises, pain, misunderstandings, and blessings which followed in our discovery. You opened your arms to each other because you are led by God's example of love and forgiveness. My life would not be complete without all of you. You are my hearts.

To our own "Sarah," our surprise blessing and daughter. When I saw you for the first time, I saw my children in you. Had we known you earlier, we would've embraced you as our own as we do now. Your presence in our lives has shown us how God's love and timing can truly grace a family and open us up to unexpected blessings. We are so grateful you came to us and for the bravery it took to take the leap of faith in trusting God to work His miracles.

To the family who raised our "Sarah." Although we may never understand your decisions, we are grateful to have her in our lives. Because of your loving home, she is a fine young woman, and we bless you and celebrate the coming of our shared daughter into our family.

TABLE OF CONTENTS

PART I - THE JOURNEY BEGINS

Genevieve Galvan Frenes

CHAPTER 1 – Sarah

It's been some time since I found out about him, my birth father, that is. I'm not sure what drives me to find him. Curiosity, I suppose. Do I look like him? Does he have the same birthmark as mine behind his right ear? Do our smiles look alike?

The father who raised me looks nothing like me, yet he is the father I grew up with. I believed he was my birth father. I never questioned the truth of what I was told, although small signs lingered along the way, like footprints on a dusty road. Like the glances and the whispers. All signs of something not right.

A few years ago, I discovered I was not my dad's biological daughter. I'm twenty-six years old. I guess I should have figured it out before now.

These inklings, these signs, led me to questions about my features, my hair, my nose. None of them look anything like my dad or my mom. My brown hair and brown eyes don't match anyone I know in the family. Both my dad and brother have blue eyes like the color of the sky. They are both over six-feet tall, and yet, I'm barely five feet.

Everyone compared me to my mom, dad, and brother. I was the oddball. Nothing ever fit when it came to my place in my family, like the missing piece of a puzzle waiting, still waiting, for placement in its proper place.

After my parents' divorce a few years ago, I learned of the *other* man, my biological father. Somewhere there is a man who may actually look like me.

CHAPTER 2 - Nicholas

I sit at my desk as my algebra students figure out the equations on the screen. One student in back squints to see the numbers and moves closer. Most of the students work at their desks and are already trained to focus on the task. I monitor their progress and behavior. My students remain quiet and productive throughout the class period.

As I look at my school email, I click on the inbox icon, and up pops something unfamiliar. The subject box reads: "An inquiry for Nicholas Aldana." I open the email and read the message.

A girl, or young woman, I suppose, Sarah Williamson asks for information about a woman named Willow Smith.

A long time ago, I knew a Willow Smith. She lived in a nearby town of Steadfield and worked at Jimmy's Pizzeria in Los Pastores, California, my hometown.

Her name sounds familiar, and I retrace my memory.

Why is this young woman contacting me? The email is formal and direct. It sounds planned out. I'm not certain what she wants with me. Usually, I receive messages about school, from Mom or Brianna, my sister, or from Sophia. I'm not used to receiving such random emails, especially at school.

I decide to leave this alone, but after ten minutes or so, I return to the subject line and contents. I read it over and over until it becomes a blur.

Intrigued, I think about this young woman, who appeared in my inbox out of nowhere. Spam didn't block her message. Spam always blocks junk mail, unfamiliar contact names, advertisements, everything, except this one message from Sarah. How did this get through?

CHAPTER 3 – Sophia

Valentine's Day was yesterday. The kids liked their presents—candy, balloons, a stuffed animal for Kaden. When I walked into the kitchen, Nick placed beautiful flowers and card on the table. He knows I love red roses, even though the practical guy in him tells him they will die. He knows I'll cherish his soon-to-be dead gift.

This year Nick acts unusual. His distant, unfocused look doesn't match the man I have been married to for over twenty years. I know men have their own moods, but around Valentine's Day? Well, it makes me wonder.

Women think of romance, candlelit dinners, flowers, candy. These little luxuries make the holiday live up to expectation. However, Nick seems engrossed in his own thoughts lately, and I wonder if he has given much thought to this special day.

I know I shouldn't think in this negative way, but my mind wanders off. *Is there someone else?* I know it's wrong for me to suspect, but some men we know haven't been the most trustworthy. I like to believe the best in everyone, but I've seen men falter, even the best of them.

Lawyers, doctors, even pastors have given in to temptation. Infidelity, lies, affairs—they've all happened to loving women. On the other hand, some of the women involved with these adulterers, their mistresses, did not have much integrity either. So I suppose this is why I question when I shouldn't. The realist in me, I guess.

Nick has never given me reason to suspect him of cheating. Yet, if something happens to my marriage, I'd feel like a fool. Yes, I'd be the fool to trust him in the first place.

Others might say, "Didn't you know?" or "Were there signs you chose not to see?" I don't want to be too trusting, but it's better to be cautious. I don't like feeling betrayed. Better to be on guard and see what happens.

CHAPTER 4 – Sarah

Time and memories have a funny way of catching up with you.

The looks, the quiet whispers. They talked about me. It's like the girl who has her skirt hiked up into her underwear after leaving the bathroom and no one wants to say, "Hey miss, you need to pull your skirt down. Your undies are showing." They look with sly eyes, faint giggles. You know they're talking about you, but no one says a word.

Embarrassment isn't what I endured during these moments. It was more of a quiet, secret humiliation.

Kindergarten is when I first knew something was wrong.

Five-year-olds are the most honest people on earth. They look you straight in the eye and speak their minds. They might not understand all of the exaggerated or incomprehensible words from their mouths or even realize the impact of what they say, but they have to say it. Why? Because their words contain the simple truth. It falls off of their lips in the way syrup falls from a bottle—all in one gooey clump, unable to separate itself, and too thick to stop at any one point. Honest truth has to be released, or the five-year-old will just bust from holding it in too long. Sort of like a helium balloon with too much helium.

Simple, honest truth does not know how to lie. It is the most direct and critical compilation of words. How do I know this? I know because my close friends, Heather and Amber, my kindergarten "sister-friends," knew about my identity before I did. They knew in the same way mediums know about your future before you do.

Mom and Dad dropped me off at school. Sometimes they came together, and sometimes separately.

Amber and Heather saw my parents from where they stood by the swings before class. They'd always glance back and forth between Mom and me. They did the same with Dad and me. After many glances and days of quiet speculation, one of them decided to speak the simple truth.

I ran to meet them. I didn't know what was coming.

"Hey, Amber. Hi Heather. What's up? I like your new backpack, Amber." I grinned at my friends.

"Thanks. Mommy bought it for me since I lost my other one." Amber grinned back.

"Hi Sarah. Umm, can I ask you something?" Heather curled her hair around her little finger.

"I guess so." I smiled, while I held onto the chains of the swing.

Heather looked at me without a hint of guile. "How come you have dark brown hair and brown eyes? Your daddy and brother's hair and eyes aren't the same color."

"I don't get it." I scrunched my eyes in confusion. "This is how God made me, silly." I kept the smile on my face.

Amber stared at me. "Yeah, they don't have your color hair, either. Theirs is super-duper light brown, almost as blonde as my Barbie. And your face doesn't look of the same as any of them. You have a heart-shaped face, like a Valentine. Their faces are round, like a ball."

Heather giggled. "Yeah, Sarah, are you sure you belong to the right family? You don't look like them. I've even heard my mommy say how different you look from everyone in your family. She just noticed. Nothing bad."

"Yeah, well..." I wanted to cry. "They *are* my daddy and brother. I don't know why I look different. I think they are mine." I didn't know what else to say, but I began to question.

Amber looked closer. "There's something not the same about all of you. I can't tell what it is, but it is definitely not the same."

"Yeah." Heather nodded in agreement.

They must have noticed my smile turn to a frown because Amber blurted out, "We don't care. We just noticed. You're our friend, Sarah. Don't be unhappy. We didn't mean to make you sad."

"We're friends for life, 'member? Once sister-friends, always sister-friends. Pinky swear." Heather held up her little finger. "Come on."

Amber held out hers and linked it with Heather's. "Yeah, it's okay if you don't look like your family. You're still the same Sarah, funny, crazy Sarah."

I looked at my friends. Although the facts of my facial features seem obvious now, in the moment, I didn't want to think about any of it. I just wanted to be loved.

I smiled and joined my little finger to theirs. "All right, sister-friends."

We held hands and ran away with giggles trailing in the wind as we lined up for class. The bell rang, which alerted us to our daily routine of lessons, arts and crafts, and recess. My sister-friends never brought up the subject of my appearance again, but their glances in the future confirmed the questions, which still remained on their minds.

My sister-friends and close family friends observed changes as I grew older. My dark hair and brown eyes, and my tiny stature existed in a world of their own. I wanted to believe what I was told, but when I looked in the mirror, simple truth spoke loud and clear. I was definitely out of place.

Although I knew my family loved me, a dark curiosity burrowed itself in my gut. The feeling stayed with me not just for months, but for many years. I wanted to push away this unknown question because I was afraid the immensity and burden of its discovery would be too great for me to bear. I buried my doubts for a long time, and did not want to scratch the surface of the discovery I somehow knew existed, yet never came to light. Until now.

*****

It's been a week and he hasn't answered. Maybe my email was too forward, too inquisitive. He probably thinks I'm some weirdo trying to scam money like many I've seen on the Internet. I know I'd think the worst in his position. He doesn't have a clue as to who I am. Do I really expect him to answer me? My doubts consume me.

I worked hard to be sure my email expressed my main points. My closest friends, Heather and Amber, read it before I sent it, and they gave me their approval.

"Yes, it reads as polite, formal, and direct, yet not too pushy." Heather handed it back to me.

I'd asked for information about my mom, although I never let on I was her daughter. I suggested places and dates Mr. Aldana might have known her, and added specific information he might remember from his earlier life with her. I signed with my married name, Williamson, so he wouldn't guess my relationship to her.

I hope he responds, yet I've accepted the possibility he might not want anything to do with her—or me. Many men in his position, one he's not aware of yet, decide to ignore the issue and forget about the others involved. I hope he won't reject me when I've done my research and looked for him for so long.

My dad, my friends, and my husband have supported me through this quest. The only one who opted out is my mom. She wants nothing to do with this situation. I don't know if it's because she regrets her choices and lies, or she doesn't want to think about the life she might have had with her former lover. Maybe it's both.

"Leave things in the past. Don't look for something that might wind up bringing pain and regret," she said.

She tried all her excuses and justifications for not telling me, but I didn't want to hear any of them.

My only regret is I may have found my father twenty-six years too late.

Most people pass each other in a mall or on the street and know they aren't related. I could have passed my father a thousand times on the sidewalk, in a store, or at a movie, and never have known he was my father.

He is a stranger to me.

CHAPTER 5 – Nicholas

Friday afternoon

The week's gone by so quickly. The eighth graders leave the last class of the day, and I set up the room for Monday. The routine is the same as it has been for over twenty years now at this middle school. My materials are organized, prepared, and neat. Papers are copied, stacks are set up in their tidy rows, ready to go, and desks are cleaned off. Everything is set, ready for next week.

I've stared at this email over and over. Once I respond, I don't know what I'll get in return, and to be honest, it makes me nervous. I'm intrigued yet cautious of what this might lead to. I remember Willow, yet it was so long ago.

Is she dead? Might they be looking for friends who knew her?

It's Friday. I'm beat, and I'm going home. Too many questions for today. Fridays and weekends are for relaxation. For family.

*****

I wake up, drenched in sweat with my thoughts racing like crazy. Questions batter my mind. Who is Sarah? *What does she want with me? Why is she contacting me?*

*****

Saturday morning

As always, I wake at six a.m., even though I don't want to. I inherited this trait from dear old Mom, the early bird. Even if I go to bed at one in the morning, I still wake up at six like a rooster.

I sweeten my coffee with French vanilla creamer, get out the laptop, read the local online paper, and eat breakfast in the quiet morning before Sophia and the kids awaken.

I wait, or I should say hesitate, to respond to the mysterious email until around eight-thirty. I finally settle on this response:

Hello Sarah,

11

I received your email. I am sorry to have taken so long to reply. I remember Willow Smith from many years ago. I have not been in contact with her since 1981. I have heard nothing of her since then. May I ask how you found me? Also, what is your connection to her? I can be reached at this address. My work email typically filters my correspondence. Many emails go directly to SPAM. I hope I can be of help to you.

Sincerely, Nicholas Aldana

I try to redirect my thoughts. I think about the email throughout the day. But in reality, I have so much to fix with our new house. I can't handle any more distractions at the moment.

The house is a disaster zone. With our move in December (we moved in on Christmas Eve—books, clothes, and Christmas tree), everything remains in disarray as I decide what to tackle first as my main project. The attic, which is nonexistent now, needs to be built. I've already cut a hole in the ceiling of the garage, taken my measurements, and reassured myself I will complete it soon. Once I start a project, I want it done right.

My grandpa taught me this work ethic: thoroughness and diligence always. I've carried his philosophy with me, though he died in 1982. He has been gone for a while, but he was my mentor. Heaven is now his home, but I still want to make him proud. I'm certain others may think this strange of a grown man, but to me, it isn't strange at all. It's my way of being the man he wanted me to be.

I work through the day, cutting and measuring pieces of wood for the attic floor and the walls in the adjoining areas. After attaching the pull-down stairs to the ceiling of the garage, I make trips up and down, bringing the materials, and gathering all of the tools I'll need. I have to complete the space very soon as the boxes and bins are still waiting in the hallway.

The email haunts me as I work.

I decide to Google the name "Sarah Williamson." I assume she's looking for information about the woman she mentioned, even though I really don't remember much about Willow.

As I grab my computer, faint memories of the past appear like Willow's picture in an old yearbook. In my mind, I look at this withered old photograph and remember faint recollections, but the past doesn't connect to the present. Names, places, events are all a blur like the colors in a watercolor painting. She's simply a memory.

I hide away in the attic where no one can find me. My family doesn't know about the strange inquiry, and I don't want to worry them.

When I click on Google and search for Sarah Williamson, I see the picture of a young muscular man, a taller woman in the middle, and a younger-looking woman to the right. The young woman has dark brown hair, brown eyes, and is short-statured. The more I look at her, the more I see the same Indian nose as my fourteen-year old, Carissa. She smiles just like my sister, Brianna, and me.

I breathe in the cold air of the attic around me. Chills run throughout my body. *This must be a dream. It can't be happening. Not after so long. Willow belongs to my distant past.*

Now, Willow reemerges in this young woman on the screen.

CHAPTER 6 – Sophia

Since Valentine's Day, Nick has been working himself ragged. He tires himself measuring and cutting wood for the attic. He's determined to get the space completed soon. He works in our freezing garage, day and night, comes in exhausted, and drags himself into bed. Although I'm concerned about him working so hard, I guess I shouldn't mind all of the time he's away from us, since many husbands leave things half done or not done at all.

Many of my friends' husbands start a project and take years to finish. Some never do. I've heard friends' horror stories about their non-productive men: a porch half finished, the stairs, which need to be fixed, but never are, a broken window, a broken tile, and on and on. Their wives never forget the things men *say* they'll do. Some even finish the job themselves or hire someone else to complete the project.

Nick has never left a job incomplete. Once he starts something, he has to finish it. Always the go-getter. I like this quality about him.

The new house has so much potential. I love the long entryway, the family room, the vast stairway. Everything about our home is to my liking.

When visitors come into the house, they enter a foyer with soaring ceilings and massive walls, covered in artwork and family portraits. In its central location, the spacious family room can be seen from the dining area and the game room. The stairway leads to the girls' rooms and their music loft, created just for their guitar and drum set, microphone stands, and amplifier.

The kitchen is my favorite room with its granite counters and large black-and-grey speckled island in the center. It is the perfect workspace for the pastries and cookies I love to bake, especially in the winter. The large pantry can store tons of food and drinks, a necessity for a family as large as ours. The shelves on top of the cabinets display plants and my "Recipe for a Happy Kitchen" plaque. It reads:

5 cups of love,
2 cups of loyalty
4 cups of forgiveness
2 cups of friendship
4 quarts of faith
and endless cups of laughter.

The kitchen is a dream for someone like me who loves to cook.

Unfortunately, with four kids and lots of bins filled with seasonal clothes for each child, plus other odds and ends, we need the attic space for storage. So Nick pushes himself each evening.

Yet, he can't sleep. I see exhaustion in his red eyes, and he complains about his sore back. He wakes up at three or four in the morning and doesn't come back to bed. I hear his shuffling feet on the tile in the hallway. He sounds like he's dragging himself around the empty house, unable to find comfort.

What could be on his mind? He's so exhausted I don't question him. I just let him be. I decide to focus my attention on Carissa, our thirteen-year-old. In a few weeks, she will be fourteen. I have two teens and two younger children. I know Carissa wants something simple for her birthday. Like sushi. Simple. Right.

CHAPTER 7 – Sarah

Two days after Nicholas's reply, I receive a second email. He wants to talk, and he has questions.

I write my response the same day. I try to explain what I know. He says he has seen a picture of me through a Google search, and he attaches the link. He seems intrigued, and not entirely clueless. Only curious.

He asks about when I was born and suggests November of 1981.

I tell him my birthday is October 5, 1981. I also explain I found him through Lorraine, my mom's best friend. In several of her conversations with my mom, I heard the name, "Nicholas." I never understood who this person was until later when Mom finally led me to the truth, around the time of her divorce from my dad.

I continue to tell him about my parents' divorce and the terrible shock of learning Steve, my dad, wasn't my biological father.

Hints about my true origins came in pieces through the years. Once, in a casual conversation with her friend, my mom was venting about my father and let the name "Nicholas" out, hinting that he was important somehow to her. She wasn't aware of my presence nearby. Of course, I figured she was somewhat teasing as she made this statement. Some old boyfriend or something of that nature.

I finally had the nerve to ask about the name I'd heard. Her friend, Lorraine, told me there had been another man in my mom's life before my dad. Although I didn't quite know what she meant by "they were involved," I was certain the name Nicholas was important. I was mortified to think he might be connected to me. Yet, it made sense when I looked at myself in the mirror and compared my appearance to my dad's.

The bitter arguments between my mom and dad, which came later, pointed to the same question. Why did their only daughter not resemble her father or her mother?

I let the idea of another father rest for years, whether out of fear of the truth or just plain denial. I'm not sure which I was more afraid of. Secretly, I longed to know where I came from since the seed of curiosity was planted by my best friends and furthered by my mom's words, but I kept pushing the idea away.

Fear held his mighty hand over my heart, telling me to stop searching. *Stay with the ones you already love. They are your family.* Although I listened to fear for a long time and wanted to believe my family was truly my family, love spoke more soundly and strongly with her words. *Find the truth, and all the pieces will come together. Your strength will help you discover the truth.*

All of the uncertainty left me fragmented, like the subject of an incomplete painting. In the crucial years before, during, and after the divorce, I craved the feeling of completeness from one who would acknowledge and embrace me as his own.

Paternity tests didn't come until several years after my parents' divorce. My heart whispered, *You need to know where you come from. You need to know the truth.* The faint whisper of truth wanted to come out, yet fear made his stand again.

Finally, my dad took a paternity test, and the results confirmed what we had both suspected and feared. Although Dad was a good and loving father, the test brought closure to a longstanding question.

As for me, this newfound knowledge changed my life in an instant and became the discovery of a lifetime. Dad is *not* my biological father. According to my mom, all indications point to Nicholas as the only other possibility.

Now I've found him.

I explain I don't wish to cause any interruption in his life. I figure he must have a family by now, and this news might upset him or his family members. I'm aware any discovery of this nature is always shocking and maybe intriguing.

I tell him I mainly want information: medical history, half siblings, information about ancestry, etc. I want to know where I come from, and I hope he'll help me.

I end the email with my phone number and send it off.

I breathe a sigh of relief. I've found him, and the dark cloud, which has hung over me for so long, seems to lift. I finally feel complete. I know a little more about who I am.

I have no idea what to expect, but I've taken the first steps.

CHAPTER 8 - Nicholas

The first time I see her on the screen, I know she's mine. Her features, her eyes, her nose, the smile. I fall in love with her. It's the same kind of love I felt upon meeting my newborn babies for the first time. This feeling brings back memories of the arrival of each of my children. Instant love. Instant pride. In this case, she's a grown woman, not small and shriveled like the others were at birth.

Had I known about her years ago, I never would have let her go. Now, twenty-six years later, all I have is a picture and a series of emails to connect me to Sarah.

I sit in the attic and stare at the bright screen in the darkness. My heart races. I hear it beat loudly in my ears like a bass drum. I'm surrounded by a swirl of white plumes as I breathe heavily in the freezing air. Although cold surrounds me, and I shiver for sheer survival, beads of sweat form on my forehead. I feel like I'm going to be sick.

Another daughter. What am I going to do? I have three daughters, a son, a wife. What do I do? Where do I begin?

My mind races on and on like a hamster going for the marathon on its spinning apparatus. I can't think. I can't breathe. I just stare and contemplate my new reality. *What the hell am I going to do?*

CHAPTER 9 – Sophia

It's Saturday. I promised to take Carissa to Santa Ava for sushi at Mountain Park.

We went to Katherine's NJB basketball game this morning. Katherine is my baby girl, well not really a baby, but my youngest daughter of eleven.

As soon as we get home, we shower and get ready for the forty-five minute drive. Marilyn, Carissa's best friend, is here with us, and soon we'll pick up cousin Kiera at the Munoz Arena in Santa Ava. My niece, Kiera, is helping her mom, my sister-in-law, Brianna, with her flourishing chair decorating business, Cozy Chair Coverings. The wedding show is coming soon, and Brianna is preparing for the big day. Her ornate displays of chair covers, colorful sashes, illuminated draping, and table decorations impress even the most skeptical customers.

In a few years, Brianna has created a sound business for herself in addition to teaching full-time at a school in Los Pastores. Who knew covering chairs could generate big money?

I've applied makeup and brushed my teeth. Nick stops me as I straighten my hair. He looks stressed again. His eyes tell me he hasn't slept.

"We need to discuss something." He uses a soft tone.

"Okay." I stare into his eyes, which are glossy and look serious.

"Is it bad? Whatever you have to tell me." My guard is already up and ready.

"Yeah, we need to talk."

I go to the closet to get my jacket. I'm already annoyed as I contemplate all of the possible bad news scenarios.

He sees my expression. "Maybe it's not the right time." He knows this because of our twenty years together. I'm sure he can read my heart and knows an alarm has already gone off in my brain—a time bomb of doubt and suspicion primed and ready to explode. He looks at me and knows.

He's right. Now isn't the time. I'm not ready for this information.

It feels like my dream about walking onto the street. I see a bus coming, only it's too late to move. I wait for the impact. I shut my eyes and blink. Suddenly I'm awake and realize, thank goodness, it isn't real. I shake off the feeling because it's only a dream. A dream can be blinked away. Anxiety and stress dissipate because I know it's only my imagination. It's not real.

Now as I look at my husband, I know this isn't a dream, and the impact of this, whatever it is, will hit me, but not yet.

"Why don't we wait until I get back from Santa Ava. I don't want to ruin Carissa's day worrying about whatever this is." I move away from him to get my purse.

"Okay." I'm sure he notices my firm tone. "Just remember I love you."

He looks at me with his saddened eyes, and my suspicions piss me off.

"Yep." I peck him on the cheek and head out the door.

I'm not good at these moments. I know this about myself. I'm not compassionate or sympathetic to men with wandering eyes or failed commitments. *Maybe this is why he's been so distant. He doesn't want to tell me this secret because he knows it will set me off.*

I feel smug in my analysis.

He knows if he makes of fool of me, I'll leave him, Catholic or not. I won't be with a man who'd break his vows. I decided long ago. No woman deserves betrayal for the love she gives her spouse.

I know if this is what has happened, my actions as a wife cannot be blamed for his adultery. Pure weakness on his part is the cause, and I don't need this in my life or my children's. Although my religion teaches divorce is not an option, an annulment is allowed in cases like this. So,

I have an option. A man of God would not take part in this activity, or so my brain tells my heart.

I need space. I hope the long drive to Santa Ava will help me forget for the moment, and this is exactly what I long for. I drive down bumpy long-forgotten streets, past vast rows of grapevines and long outstretched roads, through Lugar and nearby Floresville, then onto the freeway heading north to Santa Ava.

When we get to Akiyama's Cuisine in the Mountain Park shopping center, I try a sushi roll for the first time. I enjoy the rice and the other ingredients, but the salmon leaves a slimy feeling in my mouth, so I methodically pick it out and enjoy the lunch. I refuse to consume any food slimier than my own tongue.

When we're done, we walk next door to Dork World and poke fun at the ridiculous merchandise displayed in the store. Silly, dirty, mostly naked, little figurines I decide should be banned from children below the age of twenty. However, the girls find these odd ornaments hilarious. I'm sure their giggles can be heard in the other aisles.

I walk outside and sit on a nearby bench as I wait for them to finish browsing.

Thoughts flood my mind. *Another woman? Another woman with a child?* I imagine all of the possibilities. Yet it might be something else entirely.

I don't consider illness because he probably would have been worried and relied on me for help. But he's kept this issue a secret. Now I know why sleepless nights have become the norm, along with bloodshot eyes and a haggard expression. *Maybe his bloodshot eyes have been from crying, not from lack of sleep.*

The girls head out of Dork World. I smile and play along with the celebratory mood of the day as we continue onto the yogurt shop and then head home.

We arrive around seven o'clock. I change into my pajamas and sit in Grandma Sandra's rocking chair. I had asked for this chair after her passing since it is what I remember most about my visits with her.

She was Nick's grandmother, the mother of thirteen children, most of whom died from alcoholism before her own ninety-eight years of life ceased. *I hope her spirit will give me strength.*

I see Nicolas walk to the door, lock it, and come to me. I imagine Grandma Sandra to be my spiritual guide, my guardian angel. I brace myself on the arms of the chair and wait for the ride to begin.

"Do you want to take a guess about this?" He looks tentative.

"You have a child with another woman," I blurt out, staring blankly at him.

He stops and looks at me. I read shock. "Why would you guess that?"

"I don't know. You asked for my guess."

"The only way I know how to explain is to show you a picture. Do you want to see it?"

I take a deep breath. "Yes."

He boots up his laptop, and we wait in silence as the small computer breathes into life.

I can hear my heart beating, waiting for the moment it will break.

"About two weeks ago, on Valentine's Day, I got an email from a young woman. She was looking for another person. I thought she was looking for this woman because the lady had died. But it turned out to be something different."

I feel anxiety rising in me, like the moment before a rollercoaster jets me down a track. My palms begin to sweat, and I hold my breath.

"Willow Smith was her name. Sophia, she was beautiful. Everyone wanted her, and to be honest, I don't know what she saw in me."

Really? Is this how you start this conversation? She was beautiful? Everyone wanted her? I'm already pissed as he explains his connection to her and even more so as I look at the girl on the screen. *Where is he going with this story?*

Then, I remember the husband I know and contemplate the husband before me. This man feels like a stranger. He looks tired, confused, scared, and possibly angry. He looks just like those people on television who are interviewed after losing a loved one. His dazed appearance and indecipherable words make him appear lost.

I need to know the truth.

He shows me a picture of three people: a young man with a ball cap and a black t-shirt, a tall muscular woman with dark, straight, black hair, and a shorter woman with wavy dark brown hair.

"What do you notice?" He waits to give me time to digest it.

As I look closely, my eyes lock on the girl to the right. I'm drawn to her dark brown hair and brown eyes. I see something familiar. "The girl looks like Carissa and like your sister, Brianna, and she's your daughter." Where the words arise, I can't say, but as I say them, I am certain of their truth.

After a brief hesitation, he looks into my eyes. "Yes." He nods his head.

I take a deep breath in and try to gather the chaos in my head as he explains the story of a lady named Willow and this girl, Sarah, who is his daughter. The words spill from his mouth like pebbles hitting the floor all at once. Tiny gathering sounds blend and bump into one another until all I can hear is noise.

Tears fill my eyes as I realize how real this is, and not a dream. I wish someone would slap me hard to awaken me from the gathering storm I know is coming. My neat little world is now torn to pieces.

When his story is over, he hugs me, and I cry into his shirt.

"I'm sorry, Sophia. I'm so sorry. If I could take it back, I would. I knew her a long time ago. My life is with you and the kids. I'm *so* sorry."

He tells me over and over how much he loves me, how he never guessed this would happen, how he wishes he'd have been there for Sarah. Tears fall as he speaks.

"She's been kept from me. Gone from me, Sophia, for so long. All of this time. I feel sad, and angry, and lost. I'm so sorry."

I cry along with him. I cry for him and for me and for our children.

We go to bed early. The kids don't know anything about tonight's revelation, and for the moment, I am relieved. It's been too much for one night. I can't bear to deal with their pain, too.

I don't know if he falls asleep or not, because I know I won't sleep. I get up and walk around our house during the wee hours when silence reigns with our three beautiful princesses and handsome prince asleep soundly in their beds.

How odd. One moment in time twenty-six years ago changed my world in exactly one moment tonight. When they're young, do people think about how their actions and the consequences will affect the future? Do they realize some decisions will catch up with them someday?

I try to blink away explanation after explanation, but tears fall like soft rain on a cloudy day. I pray to God for help. *What do I do with this?* Our safe haven is not what it used to be. What once was close, complete, and safe is now shattered, odd, and disrupted. A fragmented puzzle tossed to the wind.

We've become like everyone else. Sarah is part of him and the other woman. She is now part of us, Nick and me, and our kids. *What can bring us together again? Can anything?*

Although I've known my husband forever, this child is a part of his life I never heard of or knew about. *Who is this man, my husband?*

Panic surges through me. I try to close my eyes and pray away my fears. The pacing and continual praying wear on me until finally, sometime early in the morning hours, I return to bed and give in to slumber.

I've heard God carries us in our darkest moments. His footsteps can only be seen in the sand as He carries us through life's trials and greatest fears. I want Him to carry me in this moment, but I want Him to carry me back to my *original* life, a life to which I know I will never return.

CHAPTER 10 - Sarah

Nicholas, my new dad, is telling his wife today. Ever since I found out I had a different father and began searching for him, I've prayed I wouldn't disrupt his life, his wife, or his children. I don't want to be the source of pain in their lives, yet how could I not? Their pain is a given, and I don't know the outcome.

How will his wife react? Will she hate me for messing up their lives? Will she choose to love me? And his kids? How will they feel about having another sister in their family? I can't imagine what must be going through her mind today. I mean, what would I do if I found out Luke had a daughter by someone else?

And what about my family? How will his wife feel about them? Will she ask: "Why are you finding this out so late? Why wasn't it kept a secret? How could you not have known?"

I'm so relieved to have found Nicholas, but I can only pray things go well today. God has always been my comforter. I needed Him desperately in this situation.

I walk around my big empty home and try to get my household chores done. Vacuuming, dusting, cleaning the showers, sinks. I fumble from one task to another, not really accomplishing anything.

I stop and look at my reflection in the bathroom mirror. I recognize a nervous wreck staring back at me, and she doesn't look too good.

Luke is out on the farm working his butt off, so I can't tell him what my heart is feeling. I sit here and sulk about something I have no control over. I have to wait for the outcome.

Will his wife feel bitterness? Pain? Rejection? Will she hate me for disrupting her life? Will I ruin their family? I never envisioned this part. I only thought of myself and finding my father. I never wanted to be the person to destroy something good, like their lives.

I sit and bite my nails for a while, imagining the worst. Then, hour after endless hour, I continue with my chores. I drag myself from one room to the next, and try to accomplish something.

My chores are not completed.

CHAPTER 11 - Nicholas

I dated Sarah's mom, Willow, right after high school. We worked together at Jimmy's Pizzeria in Los Pastores for about a year or so. She was a few years older, which didn't bother me. I was just nineteen at the time.

What I remember most about her is her beauty, although I never mentioned this to her. She was the girl every guy longed to have. Every move, every smile, every little glance from her was a welcome treat. Like a hyperactive puppy awaiting its master's pat on the head, the young men at Jimmy's enjoyed their treats. I'm sure she knew she aroused this reaction. She wasn't conceited, just accustomed to being appreciated.

When I pretended not to notice her, she took an interest in me. Maybe this is what attracted her—my lack of attention, the mystery. Deep down, I was flattered that an older woman liked me. An older woman equaled more experience, at least my nineteen-year-old brain thought so.

We dated for a few months. She'd been engaged previously, but she rarely talked about the situation, so I didn't bring it up. During this time, we became intimate. She was the first woman I knew "in a carnal way," as it says in the Bible. At the time, I didn't think about the potential magnitude of my actions. Only now, do I realize how naïve I was.

After a few months, we broke up. We just separated. I don't recall a fight or an argument. I don't recall much from those days. We just went our own ways. She left for Washington, and I never heard anything about her again.

In between our breakup and seeing her once on the street before she left for Washington, I was in a car wreck. After the accident, I didn't remember anyone, even my family members. It took a while to regain my recognition of friends, extended family, everyone else in my life. The concussion wiped out a large chunk of my memory. When people came up to me, I didn't know their names or connection to me.

After I recovered and could recall some events. My older sister, Brianna, told me several friends from school, including some girls, came to see me in the hospital. Some left the room crying. Their feelings were hurt when I didn't recognize them.

Although I didn't intentionally intend to harm them, I wasn't able to place them. Even if I learned their names, I didn't know my connection to them. I read sadness on their faces.

Willow might have been one of the girls who visited. Even though we had been close, I wouldn't have known her.

I still don't remember my hospital stay in Los Pastores.

A few months later, I ran into Willow again. By this point, some of my memories had returned. I spotted her as she crossed the street one afternoon. Her smile greeted me when I got close. I stopped to talk to her, and I noticed she looked different. She told me she was engaged again to the same guy, and she was pregnant.

I started to put our timeline together. I counted back the months. I wondered, yet I wasn't quite sure about the facts, but I wasn't stupid, either.

After casual small talk, I couldn't take it anymore. I asked her the question on my mind. "Is, or um—could the baby be mine?"

She shook her head. "The baby? Oh no, it's not yours. It couldn't be yours." She seemed confident of her answer, but I was still uncertain.

I half believed her, but at the same time, I wanted to step up in case the baby was mine. Youth didn't make me irresponsible when it came to family. Family was everything to me. My mom, my dad, grandpa and grandma, and sister had supported me through all the difficult times. They'd always been by my side.

She finally convinced me her baby belonged to her fiancé.

We said our farewells, and that was the last time I saw her. Over the years, I forgot about her.

She was my first experience with a woman, but now, my thoughts on life, sex, and marriage are opposite from what they were when I was a stupid teenager. I probably tried to forget Willow for this reason.

Now I see myself as a husband and a father. I can't believe I was so naïve as to become involved so fast. She was beautiful, but our relationship didn't last long. When she told me about the baby, I even wondered if she had been with me only to make her fiancé jealous. If so, it seemed to have worked.

When I saw Sarah's picture, the memories of Willow flooded back.

Now, as I lie in bed next to my wife, I know I can't change the past. Sarah is my daughter, and I want her to be part of my life, if Sophia will allow it. I can see this revelation was hard on Sophia.

She's been through so much in her life. She's known hard times, but she never mentions them to our kids. Only I know. I'm sad I've brought more sorrow to my wife, my love.

I wonder what happens from here. I pray she'll support me in whatever way she's able. I don't want to lose Sophia, and I can't lose Sarah.

CHAPTER 12 - Sophia

My eyes open to light entering through the semi-circle window over our bed. We still haven't covered it with blinds or curtains. I resist covering it at all since I enjoyed seeing the natural light in the room when we first looked at the house before we purchased it.

Now, with my sore, sleep-deprived eyes, I wish I had awakened in darkness.

The calm light of the moon soothes me.

I notice the bright moonlight throughout the night as I return to bed again and again. It comforts me with its soft glow, and I feel as if God's face shines down. I pray with His light shining on me. The night feels endless.

I finally drag myself out of bed and brush my teeth. It's early, and no one stirs.

In the part of our master bedroom we use as an office, we have an old blue couch. I sit on the lumpy, uncomfortable eyesore and close my eyes. I wish I had been able to rest, and I feel exhausted. I close my eyes again and pray.

An unexplainable calmness washes over me. I wonder if I'm in shock or truly transformed. Through the night, I've prayed. *What do I do, God?* These words, my mantra in the darkness of the long, tedious hours of worry, sadness, sorrow, revelation, have been my plea.

Compassion has always been a close friend. I've kept buried whatever grudges or hurts I've felt over the years. In this situation, I have a choice to make. Only I don't know what to do.

I feel alone because I know what Nick wants. Although I love him and want to support him, my mind and heart have to consider our children.

My decision will affect so many lives: mine, Nick's, the girls', and Kaden's. It will also affect Sarah. Knowing the impact, I'm distraught at the possibility of destroying our family, my haven.

Did Sarah's mother consider any of this when she decided to keep Sarah away from Nick? Did she ever think about how many lives would be affected by her actions? Did she know her daughter was Nick's when she left town?

I try to understand what Willow felt when she left to find another life without my husband. Now, I am forced to decide the future, not only of my life, but also Sarah's and our children's.

The anxiety terrifies me. *Where will this take us?* I hate not knowing what bringing Sarah into our lives will do to us as a family. I know Nick would be relieved, almost ecstatic, to know her. *But what about the children? Will they resent me for letting her in or forcing her out? Will there be problems along the way I can't foresee? Will they hate me one day if I agree to let her become part of us?*

The emotions don't rest well in my heart. The thought of a new person, a new daughter, in our lives *forever*, makes me cringe. Yet I wonder. *What if it could work? Can love connect us to each other?* My feelings and thoughts drift between mind and heart until I'm sick with worry.

I feel lost at sea. A sea of terrifying waves. Waves of angst, sorrow, doubt, mixed with anger and curiosity, sending me up and down in a giant ocean of emotions. I feel ill and nauseated and then relievcd and pleasant. I feel lost, just as I am sure his daughter feels when she thinks about us. She was lost to my husband, and I realize she must be in a storm of her own.

Still, the idea of letting her into our comfortable lives remains in the back of my mind. But the truth keeps seeping into my head and most of all, my heart.

This is the truth: my husband is a wonderful man. He has loved me through everything, helped me through every sorrow, and is truly a blessing in my life. How can one decision many years ago define him today? How can I judge him now when God has forgiven me for my faults over and over, never faltering in His love for me? Who am

I to judge him when God has always, *always*, forgiven me?

While I still worry about the long-term effects of accepting this new daughter to come into our world, the comfort of God's grace tells me to embrace her. *Let her in. See what happens.*

Love, in its most basic form, speaks to me. It speaks in a calm, reassuring tone, which I imagine sounds like God. I have heard others say they've heard the Lord speak. I feel desolated and forsaken. I am desperate for God to tell me what to do.

The truth continues her message to me, strong and clear, until the sun rises. Even as I sit here not knowing exactly what I want to do, I'm certain about the right thing to do. Even though the uncertainty lingers like an invisible haze, its presence is enough to make me struggle with my decision.

Nick awakens and comes to sit beside me. His body is warm from the blankets, and he perches on the arm of the old couch. I lean against his soft t-shirt, and he wraps his strong arms around me. The warmth of his body comforts me, reassuring me of his love, the closeness we share. We remain in silence for a while.

Finally, I turn to face him. "I've been thinking about all of this."

I pause for a moment. "I think you should tell the girls immediately. I don't want any secrets in our home. I don't want them to hear this news from someone else, a cousin, a friend of Sarah's, who might leak a hint or something on Facebook, Instagram, Twitter..." I pause. "I also think you should call her. She's been searching for you."

There. I said it, even though I'm not quite convinced of the wisdom of my suggestions.

He stares at me for a minute. He looks surprised. "So—you—you think I should tell the girls *now*? Today? When?"

"Today. When we get back from church."

"Are you sure? So soon?" He raises an eyebrow.

"Yes, you've told me, and they're going to know something is up with us. They're not ignorant. Anyone can tell you've been upset about something. The girls have already mentioned a few things to me, even though I didn't tell you. At the time, I didn't know. Now, I do."

"And call her today, too?"

"I don't know about when to call her, but I think if she's been searching for you, she needs to hear your voice. Don't you think? You've been gone for years. If I was in her shoes, I'd want to talk to you. I'd want to know you accept me."

He stares at me in amazement. I can tell he doesn't know whether to smile or cry or do both at the same time.

"I hadn't planned to tell the girls for a few months. And calling her? I didn't know when the right time would be or how you would react." His words stumble over each other in confusion and excitement.

Then he says, "Are you saying you're going to support me?"

"Yes." I confirm his disbelief and reaffirm my own decision. "I'm here for you. This feels like the right thing to do." As I say these words, I feel panic mixed with relief.

We prepare for Mass. I wake Raechel, Carissa, Katherine, and Kaden, and they get ready. We pack up the van and head to De Costa to go to Mass at Our Lady of Miracles Catholic Church. De Costa is about a ten-minute drive away from us, and I enjoy the beautiful countryside as I contemplate hearing God's word. We've been attending this new church periodically throughout the summer, and now we've made it our own.

As we sit through Mass, everything seems to have more meaning, more connections to our situation. At this point, no one knows about any of it except God, Nick, and me. And Sarah, of course.

I stare at Nick, who sits at the end of the row. Behind him, the sun illuminates the colors in the stained glass. Pope John Paul II is depicted with his staff in a background of multicolored fragments. The beauty of the vibrant colors comforts me, and I stare for a long while. At the same time, I ask God's help to settle my soul. I ask Him to bless us, and to help me.

The girls sit quietly. Kaden thumbs through the missalette, and Nick sits in silence. I savor this peaceful time with them. My little world of our beautiful daughters and handsome young man was a far-off dream. Now, they are the pride of my life. I realize this is one of the last moments of just "us." I'm uncertain what the future will bring to our family. Everything will change from this point on.

After Mass, we stop at the Sizzler in Eastville and enjoy our breakfast. We laugh as we eat and talk. I take in all of my surroundings and try to hold the moments suspended in my mind. I enjoy the laughter, smiles, jokes, and teasing so typical in our family. We are perfect pieces, despite our ragged edges and mismatched personalities. Always connected and aligned to one another. This is our family.

When we return home, the girls change from their dresses and high heels to t-shirts and sweats. For me, it's sweats and a warm sweatshirt. Nick hugs me and says he loves me.

"Are you ready to tell them?" I ask.

"Yes, call them in." Nick takes a deep breath as he enters our room.

I go into the living room and tell the girls their dad wants to speak with them. I try to sound casual so they won't be scared.

"I want to go in the room with Daddy, too," Kaden pleads. "Please, Mommy."

"No, *papas*, you have to stay with me. I need your help with the puzzle, okay? Remember how we love to complete these puzzles? You made me buy this big one just for you and me, remember?"

"Papas" was my nickname for him. In Spanish, little boys are called *"papas"* and little girls are *"mamas,"* loving terms of endearment, which I grew up with and passed on to my kids.

"All right, Mommy. I'll help you." Kaden's smile lights his face.

The girls look as though they think they are in trouble, but I smile and shoo them away. *Just listen to him. It'll be okay.*

They enter the room and close the door.

Kaden and I complete some of the puzzle, which has occupied my coffee table for weeks. Piece by piece, we connect the images and colors and create a picture of birds and trees and a lake. A perfect scene.

The puzzle occupies our time. I pray quietly to myself as we work together. The anxiety gnaws at my insides and pricks my brain. I transfer my energy to concentrate on the task at hand.

Kaden is also focused, matching and analyzing the colors, celebrating in his small triumphs as he discovers a match.

"I got one, Mommy. See." He points to a completed plant.

"Yes, *papas*, I see. You are so good at this." I nod my approval.

In my mind, I plead with God that everything goes well and I've made the correct decision in telling our daughters the truth. The not knowing makes me uneasy.

Just as truth spoke to me, now my daughters must hear it from their father. I know it will be difficult for Nick, but I also know my girls. I rejoice in their loving hearts. Love is the foundation of our lives, and our children are the pieces that made Nick and me complete. Love never fails.

CHAPTER 13 - Sarah

I have sisters. And a baby brother. And not just one sister, but three. When my new dad sent me a family picture, I cried, well sobbed, all day long. Their faces, their complexions. So much like mine. They actually look like me. It has been so long since I have felt part of something, especially since my parents' divorce. When I see their faces, I can see myself in them, especially in Carissa. We both have the Aldana nose.

No longer will people ask me if I'm adopted or if I'm a half-sister. I remember people, strangers even, asking questions and my own insecurity as I also wondered where I came from. The questions I asked my mom were never answered. "Are you sure we're not of mixed race somewhere down the line? Mexican? Portuguese? How come I'm so short, but you're not, and Dad and Rob are almost six feet tall?"

Sometimes when I think about it, my anger starts to build like a slowly brewing tea kettle, ready to screech at any moment. I remember how much my Washington family has always loved me. I know I've had a good life. They gave me everything I needed and supported me in my dancing, singing, and sports.

I was their girl. I was their *only* girl, and I was never deprived of anything. Always the best for little Sarah. Yet, I knew something wasn't right. I just didn't fit in my family. Now I know what was wrong.

I stare at their picture for a long time. All of my sisters have brown hair, brown eyes, and are short except for Katherine. (She must have inherited tall genes somewhere along the line.) I feel connected to their family already, more than I ever felt in my own family. The problem now is getting to know them. I see them on the screen looking so much like me, but I don't know anything about them. We are worlds apart.

CHAPTER 14 - Nicholas

Speaking to the girls will be more difficult than I can imagine. *Will they still love me? What will they think of their dad when I confess I had premarital sex? I've told them my thoughts on this subject over and over again, stressing what not to do until marriage. Here I am, Mr. Catholic-radio-on-the-way-to-work-every-morning,* telling *them my one huge mistake a lifetime ago.*

I feel awkward. My mind swirls with all these thoughts, as they walk in and sit around me.

"Um, Dad, are we in trouble or something? Why did you call this like *special meeting* in your room?" Katherine displays her usual inquisitiveness.

She's my baby girl, and I love this curiosity in her.

"Yeah, Dad, what gives? Whatever it is, I didn't do it. Carissa did." Rae smirks and points at her sister.

Yep, that's my Rae. Her full name is Raechel, the true rebel, ready to throw blame or blunt words, and not even care. Somehow, I love her more for it.

"No, I didn't. I don't even know why we're here. Why *are* we here, Dad? Did one of us eat in our room or something?" Carissa glares at Rae. "We all know how you hate it when we eat anything in our rooms."

Belligerence covers the girls' faces.

"No, no. I have something to tell you girls, and well, this is going to be hard for me."

The girls look at each other. I can tell they wonder what major news is coming their way. They know it's big.

My voice breaks, but I won't cry in front of them. Telling them the truth is hard enough without falling apart.

I tell them the story. Their eyes are fixed on me throughout. Willow, Los Pastores, Sarah, Valentine's Day. All of it. Luckily, I get through my explanation without a tear, although the lump in my throat is begging to come out.

They ask about their mother.

"What does Mom think about all of this?" Carissa's face shows her concern.

"Is she sad?" Katherine asks.

"A little, Kat. It was hard for her to hear, but she wanted you girls to know. Mom supports me. She suggested I tell you girls the truth. I'm not sure it's right to tell you so soon, but she wanted you to hear it from me, not anyone else."

The girls look awkwardly at each other. Their glances confirm their confusion with so much information at once.

Kat's eyes start to gloss over, and I wonder if I've made a mistake in confessing to them.

After a few more questions, the girls are in agreement. The verdict is in.

What Sophia suspected is correct. They're excited to have another sister. When I look up, they hug me.

"We love you, Dad."

I close my eyes and wrap my arms around my girls, my incredible daughters.

Questions begin to pour from their mouths like an erupting fountain.

"Where does she live?"

"When do we get to meet her?"

"Does she look like you? Like us?"

When I've satisfied their immediate concerns, they leave the room.

Sophia walks in. I look at her and whisper, "I love you." The boulder remains in my throat, and I swallow hard, trying not to cry.

"We have an *amazing* family. I can't believe how well they took the news. You were right. They're excited to have another sister."

I hug my wife, pulling her close. I don't want to let her go, ever.

"I didn't cry either." I smile as I pull away.

She returns my smile. "I'm glad my motherly intuition was correct."

The rest of the day, I feel a relief I haven't felt for weeks. Every time I pass Sophia, I hold her gently.

"I love you, Soph. I'm *so* grateful for my life."

"Love you, too, babe." It's her usual response, but now it doesn't seem so ordinary. Each time she says it, I give thanks for this amazing woman I married.

She's probably sick of hearing me say I'm grateful for her, my family, my life. I understand what blessing means as I think back on the past few days.

When evening arrives, I decide that I will try to call her, my daughter, Sarah. I tell Sophia and she leaves the room to give us privacy.

"Hello, Sarah?" I ask in a nervous tone.

"Hello, Nicholas—um *new Dad*. Wow, I really don't know what to call you. Is *new Dad* okay for now?"

"Sure, whatever you are comfortable with. We have a lot of catching up to do. I still can't believe you found me, us. I hope you know I never would have left you had I known about you."

"Thank you. I know the story is amazing. I'm grateful Sophia has allowed this to happen. I'm just overwhelmed by everything. I bawled like a baby when you sent the picture of my brother and sisters. I just couldn't believe it. They're so cute, and I actually look like them."

"Well, my girls know about you now, and they took the news well. They're shocked of course, but very understanding. They wanted to know more about you. We've decided to tell Kaden a little later."

"I'm so grateful to Sophia, to the kids. I can't believe we're talking to each other. It's surreal to hear your voice, but I'm so happy."

Before long, we're laughing and getting to know each other. Spunkiness and joy seem to bounce off of her voice. She seems filled with vitality. I hear echoes of my other daughters in her tone and attitude. There are moments of awkwardness between us, but I understand.

I try to focus on her every word, every detail in the hope I won't forget what she sounds like. These are my first moments with my new daughter. My eyes are filled with tears by the end of our conversation. I'm relieved she can't see me. I wouldn't want to appear weak.

I can tell she's special. This is the beginning of a relationship with someone I should have known all of her life. I feel like I've begun a journey, an adventure. What will she bring to our family?

CHAPTER 15 - Sophia

Following the initial shock, I know my life will never be the same.

Nick spoke to Sarah and says their conversation went well. Later, Sarah talked to Rae and then to Katherine.

Facebook and Instagram have connected them quickly. Sarah is learning about birth dates, trips, and celebrations she missed through the years. Her photos have begun to fill in the blanks about her friends and family. Our kids have shared information about their friends, and extended family. Soon Sarah asked to connect to the girls' friends here in Eastville. Little by little, the girls and Nick are getting a sense of who Sarah is and are trying to understand life from her point of view.

Today, I email Nick about Sarah. She's been on my mind along with the other children.

From the beginning, I decided if I supported him, I'd love Sarah as my own. No half-asterisked feelings about this situation. (Half-asterisked is my newly created clean version of the word "half-ass" which I don't like to use.)

> *"I don't want to be called a stepmother because the word has too many negative connotations. As an English teacher, I pay special attention to the hidden meanings of words, and this one has too many. I know good, even great, stepmoms, stepdads, step parents exist, but I don't want the label for myself. I hope Sarah will feel as loved as our other children. I want no division or separateness as I come to know her. I would be happy just to be Sophia to her."*

A new sense of love has emerged in me. As I come to know Sarah through Nick, a strange aura has taken over my spirit, a sense of complete love, complete acceptance I can't describe to another person. It's simply *emerged* as I learn about her past, her trials, her pain on learning of her missing father, my husband. This spirit helps me open my life and heart to her and start to understand the reason for everything we are experiencing.

Most wives might not feel this affection for their husband's child, who emerged out of nowhere, but grace is strange. It's the only explanation I have for the feelings I have about welcoming Sarah into our world. Grace.

I believe this spirit was born through struggle as I've encouraged Nick let go of the past and the anger. His disillusionment and pain will never go away completely, but the love he can give to his new daughter might help ease his own resentment of her parents. He can now look forward instead of remembering his past with regret. Even I can't understand the loss Nick feels, but I know he's better than his resentment and anger. His new self isn't the man I know and isn't the man I hope will emerge from this situation.

Carissa is having a hard time with her newfound sibling. Since hearing about her big sister, she hasn't slept through the night. She's much like me in terms of keeping her emotions to herself. I have to pry at her with a chisel to get any information she keeps hidden and locked away for safe keeping.

So now, a week since the others spoke to Sarah, Carissa still seems to be struggling to grasp all of this.

I walk upstairs to her room and lie on her bed next to her.

We decorated her room in purple and lavender with "Twilight" memorabilia and the famous Taylor Lautner. Of course, she has no fully clothed pictures of this mega-hunk star. So, with his solid six-pack abs staring in my face, I try to ignore what I call "the Shirtless Man," try to gain focus, and begin to chisel away.

"So how are you with this...situation?" I study her face for a clue.

Carissa shrugs. "Uh, I don't know. I'm just sort of creeped out. I guess the fact that someone else looks like me is sort of—well, weird."

"Yeah, I guess it would creep me out, too. But don't you think it's sort of intriguing? I mean the timing and all?"

Carissa looks at me. "What do you mean by the timing?"

"Well, think about it. I met your dad in the fall of 1982. Sarah was born in October of 1981, right?"

She nods. "Yeah, what makes it interesting?"

"I'll tell you, Carissa. God gives us free will, and we make our own choices, but I believe He is present and helps us along the way. When I was a high school senior, I wanted so much to get on with my life. To make my own decisions. I planned on moving away for college, like far, far away, and never coming back. I wanted a life of my own. I didn't want to have to deal with my life as it was at the time, all the issues I couldn't control. I met your dad and we immediately started dating. I stayed here with him until I graduated from college. I never would have stayed for any other reason."

"So how does that connect with Sarah?" Carissa frowns.

"If Dad had known about Sarah when she was born, do you think I'd have stayed with him? Do you think he'd have stayed with me?"

"No, probably not. I know I wouldn't have."

"I'd have thought your dad having a kid at nineteen or twenty was way too heavy for me to handle. Simply too much. I didn't want kids that young, nor would I have stayed with someone who had a child then. Life was complicated enough to take on the additional responsibility. Also, I'm sure your dad would have wanted to be part of her life. He is a great father to you and your sisters and brother. He would have been young, but he'd have been involved in some way, don't you think?"

Carissa looks thoughtful. "Yeah, I know what you mean. If she had come to us at another age, like ten or twelve, it might have been hard on all of us, being young and not understanding her side of things. We might have been jealous, too, because we were little."

"Yes, I've thought about it too. Now, she's an adult. She doesn't have the stress of having to choose between her parents and us, and the normal drama of separated families, because she has her own adult life now with Luke. So this transition is a little easier on all of us, don't you think?"

"Yeah, it seems right in terms of timing, but it's still a little weird."

"Yes, I know. I think how different my life would have been without your dad, without all of you. I was a loner, a workaholic. If I'd gone away, I don't think I would have married or had kids, just worked and worked until it filled all my hours. I wouldn't have wanted to get involved with anyone back then."

My daughter looks surprised.

I know I need to reassure her. "However, when I met your dad, everything changed. They say love transforms people. I'm certain this is true for me. Your dad was so connected to his parents, to his family. I knew he'd never leave the Los Pastores area. So I decided to commit myself to him, and it was the best decision I ever made. I never would have had you and the other girls or Kaden. It's strange how things work out, don't you think? I've considered all the possibilities. Everything in its proper time."

"Yeah, I know what you mean. I'll talk to Sarah soon. Really, I will, but I just don't know when it'll be the right time. I think I need more space. I don't even know what I'll say or talk about with her. It still feels weird right now. Everything seems like a dream or something."

"It's okay. Take your time. I'm sure she understands. This is a big change in our lives. She seems to be very sensitive and grateful for all her new siblings. She was excited to learn about you. I know she feels good to be part of our family."

"So—are you sure you're okay with all of this, Mom? I mean, does it bother you? Sarah coming into our life?"

"Well, I'm not 100 percent back to normal. There's a lot to think about. Like the life Dad had before me. It's the hardest to understand and accept. He had a life with someone else, and she loved him. It isn't easy. In all these years, I've never considered any of this. I'll feel better in time, but I'm okay for right now. It is a big change for all of us, but I have faith everything will work out."

I kiss her forehead and stroke her hair.

"Love you," I whisper.

"Love you, too, Mom," Carissa replies.

CHAPTER 16 - Sarah

Change is the only word to describe my life. I am completely changed, impacted by my new family.

I met Raechel or "Rae," *new Dad's* eldest, well, now second eldest, daughter. She's sixteen, crazy, and forward. I thought *I* was loud. She outdoes me in a heartbeat. She's boisterous, to the point of outspokenness, much like me. In fact, when *new Dad*, described her to me, it sounded like the description others use for me.

His response was, "There can't be two of you in the same room."

Little sister, Katherine, is sweet and cute, very bubbly, and eager to learn about everything and everyone. She says the other two pick on her, and I guess I'll have to be her big sister and protector now and then.

As for the other two, Carissa has texted me. It's a small step, but still no phone call. She seems like me when it comes to private matters, quiet, a little reserved about spilling everything, and yet, polite and attentive. This seems to have affected her the most. I'll have to let her know I'm here and ask her to be patient. I've waited this long to meet my new dad and all of them.

I haven't met or spoken to the little guy, Kaden, yet. I can't believe I have a little brother. My other brother, Rob, and I are very close, but he's still a guy. Sometimes he'll open up to me. Other times, I have to try to figure him out. Typical brother, but I love him. Now, I have two.

I don't know how Rob feels about my new family. He's never said anything hurtful or critical, but maybe he doesn't want to hurt my feelings. I hope he doesn't think he's losing me, because it was always Rob and me. We've been inseparable as siblings, even as we got older. When others suggested he and I weren't related, I loved him more because he could love me without thinking twice about who I was. I was his sister, and nothing could change this fact.

I imagine it must be awkward for him to deal with my finding my new family, but he doesn't say much. Still a guy, always a guy.

Luke, my husband of two years, has been affected by all of this, too. He listens patiently and wants to be part of my journey as he tries to figure out who is who in the new list of family members. I can't believe how supportive he has been. My parents always loved Luke, and I know my new family will be charmed by his friendliness and down-to-earth spirit. He hasn't spoken to *new Dad* yet, but I'm anxious for them to talk.

As for *new Dad,* he seems very understanding. It's so odd to be sort of stuck in between two families. In fact, *new Dad* suggested we get together sometime soon. I've only shared a bit of my experience of my new family, with Mom and Dad.

New Dad listens with such patience. I have spoken to him about meeting him and my new family in person. We have a plan in the works. I'm so excited.

CHAPTER 17 – Nicholas

It has been a few weeks since I first spoke to Sarah, and I already feel like I know her. However, I'm still learning about her.

She's at the hair salon in her hometown, Cloverston. We're texting on the phone, just chatting about whatever's on our minds.

"I have something to tell you," I text, "and I have to tell you before you come. It's important."

"What is it? I asked my hair dresser to stop."

"Well, it's very important." I smile as the words flow from my fingers.

"What is it? I'm freaking out here. Is something wrong? Have I done something wrong?"

I know I've crossed the line. I text, "Oh nothing. Just kidding."

I've made a mistake. A big mistake.

She doesn't text back. I start to worry.

After half an hour of waiting, she finally responds.

"Oh, so NOT funny. You scared me. I have hives. I'm sweating, and by the way, my hairdresser thinks you're an ASS."

Apparently her hair dresser watched our conversation as it happened on her phone. *Someone in Cloverston, Washington, thinks I'm an ass.* I didn't expect the joke to result in such drama. I should have thought before sending the message. It's still too new, and she doesn't know me well yet. Man, I feel bad.

I quickly apologize.

She can't know I'm the first one to make a smart-ass comment—the first jab, the first putdown (in a kidding way). My other kids recognize when I start my stream of quick-witted jokes until they can't take it anymore. The girls roll their eyes and sometimes walk out of the room, but I know I'm funny. The boy gets my humor, and once in a while, if I'm lucky, the girls do, too. Sarah has a lot to learn about her *"new"* dad.

The other day, I picked up six-year-old Kaden early from school since I had an early release day. He was with me when I received a call from Sarah. He asked who was on the phone, and I let him speak to her. Afterward, Kaden was a little confused, but he understood he had another sister in his life. He hasn't asked any other questions yet, but I'm sure there will be some. He's still little, but he's sharp. I know he'll pick my brain in the next couple of months.

After the trauma, Sarah forgives me, and we discuss meeting. I've asked Sophia if this is okay with her. Although she's a little hesitant about a date, she's okayed the plan.

Sarah will arrive in a few weeks on March twentieth, and we plan to surprise the kids. I keep hinting to Sophia that Sarah would like to talk with her when she's ready.

Sophia says she'll call Sarah soon. I can tell Sophia finds the idea awkward.

I feel as though I've been married to Sophia forever, but I know I've hurt her. Maybe she doesn't want to speak with Sarah, or maybe doing so will make it too real for her. Hearing an actual voice to compare to her husband could be what she's hesitant about. I'll just have to wait and see and hope she comes around. She is the only one who hasn't talked to Sarah.

Carissa called Sarah a few days ago. Carissa looks the most like Sarah, and I think this seems strange to her. When I first showed the girls Sarah's picture, Carissa looked as if she'd seen a ghost, only the ghost looked like her. She didn't indicate it bothered her, but since she was the last to connect to Sarah, I think it had an impact on her. She seems better now.

As for Sophia, I hope she and Sarah get along well. Most people warm up to Sophia quickly although my wife tends to keep her distance before knowing someone well. I hope Sarah is patient.

CHAPTER 18 – Sophia

Well, the time has come to speak to her, my new daughter. It sounds strange to say this out loud because I'm not really related. I decided from the beginning she is mine, just like my other daughters and son. When anyone sees our three daughters, they are clones of each other.

Before I call her, I text her so she'll know.

She responds. She awaits my call. I can tell she's eager to meet me. The kids have told me so, and her quick response confirms this.

The kids have accepted her. Carissa finally came around. They talked the other night. Kaden asked about his other sister, Sarah. He's curious and wants to meet her. Now, it's my turn. It's time for me to be brave, just like the kids.

After a long hot shower, I sit on the old blue couch, close my eyes, take a deep breath, and call her cell phone. It's dark as I look out the French windows of the office. In the quiet, I await the sound of her voice. I take a deep breath as the ring continues. Anxiety taps me on the shoulder. *What's going to happen?*

"Hello. Is this Sophia?" I hear her voice at last.

"Yes, it's Sophia. How are you? I'm sorry I've taken so long. It's been a little crazy, you know."

"I totally understand. I'm so glad to finally talk to you. I just can't believe how kind everyone has been to me, considering the circumstances."

"Well, it was a surprise for all of us, but you know, sometimes there are reasons why things happen as they do. I think we all see this as a blessing, and we're glad you found your dad, and us."

By this point, I hear Sarah crying on the other end. My own tears fall as I listen to her gratitude for my family's love and acceptance of her. I sit and weep with her, allowing her to release emotions from this ride she's been on. She has waited a long time. I hope my silence will allow her to be honest about whatever feelings she's stored up. She says she's worried about the disruption she brought to our lives. She so wants things to be normal for all of us. She says this, although she knows how shocked we must have been and how difficult to handle the discovery has been for our family.

In her voice, I hear tenderness, she sounds almost child-like, as though she needs reassurance. Although she's twenty-six, she seems younger, vibrant, and honest about the way she sees us. She refers to my husband as "Nicholas" or "new dad." She sounds awkward as she speaks these words. I assume she still thinks of the other man who raised her as her dad and feels guilty using the term for someone else.

She describes what she knows of the kids, her brother and sisters. How excited she is to have others who look like her.

I feel shivers go through me as I remember the first picture I saw of her—my Carissa appearing in her face. Nick was so evident in her features, I had no doubt her parents must have known Steve was not her biological her father. I leave this information out of our conversation, but she adds she still wants her parents' explanation.

I can tell she feels uncomfortable about her parents' past actions. She speaks about the endless unknowns in her history. Secrets seem to find a way out. In time, nothing remains hidden.

I'm certain her mother and Steve never suspected their knowledge of Sarah's identity would someday come to light. I wonder if maybe he hadn't shared in hiding it, and if it was only her, Willow.

The revelations from relatives, cousins, and even friends' human mistakes have impacted the way I see the world. It never matters what appears to look truthful in individuals, because all of us are capable of sinning. No one is without flaws, including me, but some secrets are just too big to stay buried.

I sympathize with this young woman trying to find her roots and make sense of her discovery. I empathize with Sarah as she speaks of what she now knows to be the truth of her early life and how unsure she felt about her place in her family. Her need to be part of something bigger than herself comes through every word she utters. She needs stability and love. Even though it's clear she comes from a good family, she needs something more. And now she has it.

I knew we needed to talk before her visit, which is in about a week. I don't want her to feel strange or out-of-place when we meet in person. No awkward beginnings for our new family. Our situation is awkward enough. I want our reunion to feel natural, as though she's visiting old friends.

We speak for about an hour. By the end, I have a better sense of who she is as a person. Not a complete understanding of her, but a piece, a bit of who she is. My knowledge of her isn't complete, but it's a beginning. She'll soon come home to us.

CHAPTER 19 – Sarah

I'm on my way. It's been a long couple of days since leaving my home in Cloverston. Luke is on his way to Ireland for a farmers' convention. I wish he could be here with me, but maybe it's better I meet my new family alone for the first time. I'm such a nervous wreck. I'd probably make him nervous if he had to listen to me on the whole drive.

My mind is scattered as I pass city after city on the freeway. *New Dad* didn't want me to drive alone. He wanted me to fly or have someone drive me to Eastville. I told him I would be all right. He's protective of me, which feels nice yet strange at the same time.

I've always been my own person. Very independent. I was raised to do things for myself. This is who I am. His desire to protect me is so sweet, but I'm not one to be told what to do, by anyone. I have a great deal to learn about him. And he has a lot to learn about me, too. He'll figure out how independent I am eventually.

Excitement and uncertainty swirl together as I think of what to say to them. *New Dad* wants some time alone with me, and I, too, want to see him up close and have him all to myself. My siblings, Rae, Carissa, Katherine, Kaden, will all be there. Billy, Rae's boyfriend, will also be with us. He began texting me not long after Rae and the girls did. He's the add-on big brother of the younger girls and best bud to the little guy.

I could tell Billy was a good guy from the start—a hunter and nature lover, much like Luke. He knows about our secret. We're going to surprise the girls and Kaden. Rae will hate it. He knew about our meeting before she did. I can't wait to see her expression.

By the time I arrive at their home in Eastville, I'm exhausted, excited, and starving. It's close to eight and already getting dark. Their blue two-story home is at the end of a cul-de-sac and rests right at the corner of the street. It's quiet as I near the door to ring the bell. I can feel my heart pound through my sweater like I've been running five grueling miles uphill. My sweaty palms will feel gross if he holds my hand. *Will he hold my hand? What do I do when I see him? Hug him? Kiss him? Or say, "Surprise"?* All these thoughts cloud my mind. There's no going back now.

Through the two rectangular panes of glass in the door, I see a blurred figure approach. The person would be unrecognizable even if I did know him. The slow click of the deadbolt. It's him—*new Dad.*

When he opens the door, we are both speechless.

"*New Dad*? So glad to finally meet you." I extend my arms for a hug.

He studies me, taking me all in, and then embraces me with the warmest hug I've ever received.

"I can't believe you're here. I never would have let you go. Never."

He hugs me again until I feel like I might not be able to breathe.

"Oh, it's so good to finally be here. I didn't know how this would end, but I'm so glad to have found you."

I have been waiting so long to meet him, and here he is. He continues to gently stroke my hair. As if in disbelief, he holds me like a child, and embraces me again and again. Our tears mingle. Although this place is different from my own surroundings, something tells me a part of me is now home.

CHAPTER 20 – Nicholas

The apprehension and the suspense are killing me as the hours pass awaiting Sarah's arrival. The girls and Kaden know nothing except we're going out to eat dinner. I pretend to take a nap and slowly get ready. Sarah's on her way, but we don't know exactly when she'll arrive. It will depend on the traffic. Her updates arrive from time to time.

Finally when she's about fifteen minutes away, I tell Sophia to take the kids ahead to Bryan's Burgers since they're starting to gnaw on each other, ravenous at this point. I tell Sophia I love her, and she heads off with the clan. The only one who remains is Billy, our videographer for the evening. I asked him to stay and film our first meeting. I knew it would be something I'd treasure for the rest of my life. He gladly agreed, and I think it made him feel special to be included since Rae has made him part of the family already.

When Sarah arrives, Billy hides behind the wall near the game room. I open the door, laughing and crying at the same time.

She exclaims, "*New Dad.* Nice to finally meet you."

I hold her in a tight bear hug and won't let her go until she motions she can't breathe. I look into her eyes. "I never would have let you go. Never." Again, I embrace her as she buries her face in my chest. I hold her like I'm going to miss her for a thousand years if I even let her out of my sight again.

I finally release her, and Sarah greets Billy, who's been crying behind the video camera as he filmed our emotional meeting.

"Is that you, Billy?" Sarah tries to peek behind the camera.

"Yeah." He wipes his tears and fumbles with the equipment. "Yeah. Hi, Sarah."

"Aww, you, too. Look at us. We're a bunch of blubbering crybabies. It's so good to meet you." She reaches to hug him.

"It's good to finally meet you, too." Billy tries to hug her without dropping his camera.

After a few minutes of talking about her trip, we agree we're starving, so we head off to Bryan's Burgers.

"I know some kids who really would like to meet you." I smile in anticipation of their reaction.

"Yeah, I can't wait to see Rae's face. She's going to hate me for knowing about all of this. I love it." Billy grins.

By the time we arrive, the Aldana crew has ordered and is sitting down. Sophia waits for us by the door.

"Hi, Sophia." Sarah wraps her arms around my wife. They hug and then turn their attention to the kids at the table. Sarah motions to the family, although they are still unaware.

The kids look toward us. All of their focus shifts to Sarah. Although it takes a few seconds to recognize the new person, they jump from their seats, arms already spread as she walks toward them. A giant group hug ensues in the middle of Bryan's Burgers amid the customers, who glance with startled looks, and "aww" smiles for the reunion they're witnessing.

All of our daughters, Rae, Carissa, Katherine—and Sarah, hug and cry. Little Kaden tries to squeeze in, and his eyes light up as he recognizes his new big sister.

"I want to hug her, too," he demands. The girls laugh and let him into the circle.

As we order and sit down, we continue to stare at her, this young woman who's travelled so far to find me and now, our family. In many ways, she looks the most like Carissa, yet other features resemble Katherine and Rae with her darker hair and eyebrows. The shape of her face and nose are like Carissa's.

At first, the kids sit and eat and smile across the table at Sarah. I'm sure they are determining how much Sarah resembles them. They grow comfortable with each other and giggle the night away.

"You jerk, Billy. You knew about this? Such a jerk." Rae crosses her arms and pouts.

"Yeah, I knew *before* you, Rae. Ha." He beams.

Rae gives him a quick punch, her usual rough "I hate you right now" self.

He rubs his arm with a big grin on his face.

"Love it," he says.

Soon, the manager, a young guy about thirty or so, asks about all of the commotion. As we tell him our story, his face reflects our own shock when we found out about Sarah. He congratulates us, and then tells a story about an older gentleman and daughter who came into the restaurant several weeks before.

This man, Tom, was probably in his seventies and had just come to find out about a daughter, about whose existence he had never known. Since he was a regular breakfast customer, the manager had made friends with this man. He'd listened to Tom's story, and it reminded him of ours. Tom had never known about the daughter born to his previous girlfriend. Friends of the family had been contacted by a woman looking for him. Eventually, a connection was made via the Internet. The woman, now in her fifties, came in with Tom, and he introduced her to the manager as the daughter he had never known.

When I think about Tom's story, I wonder how many other fathers, daughters, sons, are looking for each other due to lack of communication from a former girlfriend, wife, or lover. Tom's daughter's locating him is a true miracle, just like the miracle of Sarah sitting here with us in California.

At the end of the evening, we take a family picture with all of our kids, right in the middle of Bryan's Burgers. It's late, and the last remaining customers stare at us a bit, but we don't care. We savor this memory.

CHAPTER 21 – Sophia

I could not sleep last night. Worry and exhaustion destroyed my ability to reason, and I spent the night thinking about all the "what ifs." *What if Sarah is strange? What if she doesn't get along with the kids? What if she is nothing like us at all? What if she wants to destroy Nick and our family? What if she is angry?* These would have been somewhat normal concerns about any stranger coming to stay with us, but I don't think of Sarah as a stranger. Through our conversation and texts, I've become comfortable with her, so I didn't expect to have these fears before she arrives.

In the two weeks since we set Sarah's arrival date, I've decorated the living room with wall hangings, portraits, special knickknacks and family treasures.

Nick told me, "Go shopping." He attached no financial limits, so I couldn't believe what I heard. In our entire marriage, he's never uttered these words. He's not terribly cheap, but he's always been frugal in order to provide for our family. We just undertook the added expense of the new house and the remodel of the garage. I'm usually the one who does most of the shopping with his voice in the back of my mind saying, *"Do we really need this item?"*

I wasn't going to pass up this opportunity, however. So, I shopped like someone who had won the lottery.

Since we moved in last December, most of my time has been devoted to unloading boxes and organizing, along with the rest of the busy life of school and housework. I arranged our room the best I could without a bookcase for the four hundred or so books we previously housed in the large built-in bookshelf in our old house. I bought new bed linens with matching pillows in brown, light green, and neutral colors. We painted the girls' rooms, hung up artwork, and arranged furniture.

Last night, I mopped the tile floor at midnight since any time before seemed to be useless with four kids trailing in and out of the house. Dirty feet, muddy shoes—the dirt just keeps coming in. The kids thought I was going crazy since they didn't know I was trying to keep the house clean for a surprise guest.

All they saw was their mother scolding them for leaving dishes out, dirt on the floor, towels unhung, etc. I wanted the house to be immaculate and homey for Sarah as she enters our world. So when I lay down to sleep, and sleep never came, I was physically and spiritually exhausted. Three or four hours of solid sleep are all I got last night. I tossed and turned. Finally, I got up and walked around the house, inspecting it one last time, and hoping to tire myself out.

But anxiety whispered the night away. All I could think of was the stranger who was going to enter our lives. *What if she feels awkward around us? What if she creates problems with our kids, with me, with Nick? What if she's crazy and not related to us in any way? What if she made up this story just to get into our home? Is it a game to her? What if she hurts our children?*

I am allowing her into our lives. She's related to Nick by blood, but without my blessing, none of this would happen. I knew my concerns were ridiculous even as they flew around my exhausted brain. I knew the facts were accurate. Yet, anxiety kept pestering me like a mosquito on a hot summer night. I couldn't get rid of her.

I first glimpse Sarah at the entrance of Bryan's Burgers. The moment I see her, I realize my anxiety was for nothing. I'd ordered our food and told the kids that I'd wait for our order. They're tired and famished as they wait at a long table near the back of the restaurant. I'm glad they're in this location because they won't see Sarah arrive.

She walks behind Nick. I can barely see her. (She's so tiny.) She runs around him to greet me warmly and falls into my arms like a young child. I instantly feel a connection. All my fears subside and then melt away as I see features of my own daughters in Sarah.

We join the kids and share a group hug. Then we enjoy our food and try to relax. We're all on such a high it seems I might have another restless night tonight.

We return to the house, and I change the sheets on Katherine's bed so Sarah might have her own private room with an adjacent bath.

As she gets settled, I finally ask the question heavy on my heart. "So, how was your mother with all of this—meeting us and all?"

Her response is hesitant. "Well, she didn't like the idea of my coming, but I know she'll be okay. She's my only mom, and she sort of reminded me about it before I left."

I certainly want to respect their relationship. "I see. Hopefully, she won't feel too badly. We're glad you are here, especially your dad."

"Yes, I know." She smiles.

"Well, I'll let you get some sleep. Goodnight." I turn to leave.

"Goodnight."

A few minutes later, Nick and I settle into bed, and I can hear the quick patter of feet. I assume one of the girls wants to be with Sarah since Kaden crashed once he showered and was tucked in. We lie in bed and listen to giggling and chatter. For the first time in a long while, with my home at peace, I fall asleep.

CHAPTER 22 - Sarah

What a rush. My brother and sisters all welcome me into their family, along with Sophia and *new Dad*. It's one thing to see siblings in a picture, but in real life, it feels eerie to see our resemblance, especially quiet Carissa. I spend most of the first night getting to know my sisters.

I peek into Carissa's room. She's the hesitant one, so I immediately try to get to know her. Katherine and Rae trail in to join us.

I have so many questions. "So what are you into? Sports? Any clubs?"

To my surprise, Carissa answers first. "No, I'm mainly just school. Not into the jock or social scene. Just myself."

"Any boyfriend yet?" She hasn't mentioned one in any of her texts.

"No, the boy scene is just not me right now. I'm not the girl scene either." Carissa grins.

"Ha. Okay, then." I laugh. "What about you, Rae?"

"I love singing, choir, performing. Man, I just love it. I've played the guitar forever, Music is my life."

"What about you, Katherine? Anything favorite to do?"

"Well, I love basketball, and sometimes I like to sing and mess around on the keyboard. I like hanging out with my friends too."

"Basketball? Are you the athlete in the family? What about Kaden?"

Katherine smiles. "Yeah, he likes soccer and sometimes basketball. He's little, and well, I don't know exactly what he likes."

I've only had Rob, my younger brother, in my life, but to have sisters is quite a different experience. And to now be their big sister. I just love the idea. I know I'll remember this moment forever.

We giggle into the night and laugh until we fall asleep. We all scatter around Carissa's room and find places to snooze for the night. To a casual observer, it must appear pretty messy, but for me, it's just perfect. Like it was meant to be.

*****

I spend today, Wednesday, with *new Dad*, sitting out by the pool and answering his questions.

"So tell me about how you and Luke met."

"Well, we basically met through some friends in college. You know, just all of us together at dinner, laughing and having a good time. Once he finally got the nerve, he asked me out a few months later. You know what our first date was? Surfing. Who takes out a first date on the waves? I swear, I didn't know what I was doing, but he had a good laugh."

"Well, maybe he wanted to trap you in the deep ocean, so you couldn't escape." *New Dad* laughed.

"I have to admit, it was original." I smiled.

"From what you've said, he seems to have established himself well with his farm and everything. Sounds like a good person. It's nice to know my firstborn is treated well by her husband. That's important, you know." He took a drink of his Crystal Light.

"Yes, I know. I was sort of nervous to get married at first. Well, Luke is such a charmer. I can't wait for him to meet all of you. He's been part of this journey since even before the paternity test. Great supportive person."

New Dad nods. "Good guy."

Later in the evening, after Sophia makes dinner, he takes me to his Back to School Night at his middle school in nearby Los Pastores along with Rae, Carissa, and Katherine. *New Dad* has worked at this school for about twenty years as a math teacher. I can tell the parents and students enjoy his personality. My sibs and I walk around the campus. We meet Sophia's cousin, Jessica, the ASB teacher for the school, and some of *new Dad's* colleagues. Once the initial shock is over, they have questions, of course. But, we don't stay in one place for long. The girls are excited to be with their new big sister.

*****

Tonight, Thursday, there's a barbeque. The occasion is partially to introduce me and also to celebrate Rae's seventeenth birthday. Among the guests are Raechel's friends, Kelly, Billy, Juan, Rianna, Nancy, and others. Sophia's mom and dad, Grandma Sally and Grandpa Julio, *new Dad's* mom, Grandma Alice, and *Tia* Brianna, and *Tio* Benito and their families also come.

I have even more new family members.

When they walk into the house, *Tia* Brianna stops and stares at me. "Oh, my gosh. They told me we looked like twins. They weren't kidding." She gives me a great big hug and keeps staring at me. It felt like I'm looking in a mirror.

Now that we're finally face-to-face, I realized everyone was correct. *Her nose, the shape of her face, her hairstyle. We're so similar.* Even our stature is almost the same— about five feet tall, maybe if we stretch. *Tia's* a bit taller, I'm told, but it's hard to know for sure since she never goes anywhere without her four-inch high heels.

Grandma Alice greets me with an album filled with their family history.

I sit on the couch beside her, and she points out the names and connections from the past. These people represent my past, too.

Tears fall as I look at all of the names of people who are connected to me, but whom I have never known.

Grandma Alice and I exchange lots of hugs. Raechel's friends from Eastville High hug me, too.

Carissa had invited her closest friends, Marilyn and Angelina, to meet her new big sister—me.

Billy arrives with the rest of the kids. He says he's heard my mom's name before. Billy's dad, William Sr., or "Will" as he likes to be called, told him about a woman he grew up with in Steadfield, a town about ten to fifteen minutes away from Los Pastores. Her name was Willow Smith.

New Dad hears this, and he tells Billy to invite his dad over.

When Will hears about this connection, he's stunned. Turns out my mom, Willow, and Will were good friends throughout high school. When he learns about me, Will tries to piece together the entire story. None of us can believe this amazing coincidence. It is definitely a small world.

Later that evening, the family tells me they bought midnight premiere tickets to *The Hunger Games*, one of my favorite novels. Most of the family has also read the trilogy. We're ecstatic about seeing the opening.

Sophia has bought all of the girls a *Hunger Games* t-shirt, and she includes me along with the others.

Even though we're exhausted, the movie is definitely worth all of the hype and attention.

*****

Sophia and the family have scheduled time away so we can all travel to L.A. for Katherine's basketball tournament. We're able to sleep in a bit this morning, before heading off to L.A.

We stay at Embassy Suites near LAX. *Tia* Brianne's family and Grandma Alice stay with us and attended the tournament. Later, *new Dad* introduces me to his *padriño* and *madriña* (godparents), Tommy and Betty. They embrace me as well, and I can sense they are genuine. Tommy, with his grand stories and funny humor, livens up the conversation as we relax in the hotel lobby.

I sit in the midst of all of these new people who have embraced me without knowing me. I can't believe it, and yet, I feel part of something special.

CHAPTER 23 - Nicholas

I feel rejuvenated. For a long time, my profession has left me feeling tired and burnt out as I trudge through meaningless meetings and endless evaluations. Basically, I feel stuck in a teacher's nightmare. I work in a school defined as not meeting standards for the kids, even though we teachers all know the truth. Our kids are learning, and we have good, even great teachers here. I never feel like what I do is good enough for the evaluation teams, the clueless people who wander into our classrooms, who know nothing about the profession of teaching.

Now Sarah has come to us, and I feel like a new person. I feel alive, excited and proud of this daughter I have gained. How courageous she is to come by herself, without Luke. She's met endless friends and family with such grace. This week has been an adventure for everyone.

Each time I look at her, I see my other daughters, yet I know she was raised by others, the people who kept her away from me. I try not to get too upset. I don't want to hurt Sarah or to condemn those who separated us, but no one knows the hatred I feel. The overwhelming sense of loss stirs inside me when I think of the many years I didn't know about her. I can never regain them. No one can understand except me.

Sophia tries to see my side of things, but she tends to forgive more easily than I do. She tells me to look forward and to think of the memories we'll make with Sarah and Luke. These can't be taken from me.

But, what about the twenty-six years' worth of memories stolen from me?

I smile for the kids, for Sarah, for Sophia. I smile to keep my anger from rising and exploding on everyone.

Now she's real and up close. I don't know how I can let her go again. *What happens from here?* She'll go back to her real "dad," the one who probably suspected she wasn't his, and her mom, who for whatever reason, kept Sarah from me.

We arrive back home from L.A. I can't bear all these emotions anymore. On the outside, I appear calm, but within, a storm is brewing and ready to hit hard. In L.A., I asked Sarah for Willow's number in an effort to bring closure.

Sarah seemed hesitant, understanding, but also concerned.

"Does Sophia know what you're planning? Do you think this is a good idea right now?"

Sophia doesn't know. I have the number, and I will tell my wife. No more secrets. That's a promise.

CHAPTER 24 – Sophia

It's Sunday, and we're back home from L.A. after three days with Sarah.

Nick tells me how he's feeling, how angry he is. He's seen Sarah in person, and wonders how this could have happened to him. Why? The question no one has the answer to or will be able to answer to his liking. I suspected somewhere along the line we'd hit this point of anger, the disappointment, and then the rage.

This week's gone by so well with family and friends. We've shared lots of smiles and warm feelings. I didn't anticipate he'd want answers now, while Sarah's still here with us. He tells me he'd like to speak to Willow if it's okay with me.

I'm surprised by his curiosity since he's never mentioned contacting her before. He reassures me he loves me. I was the one he chose, not her. I believe what he says, but I still wonder.

What is he going to discover when he calls her? Will this affect his relationship with Sarah? With me?

I suspect another wife might have blown up at his need for contact. Maybe even thrown whatever was in reach at him.

Really? Call her after this wonderful visit? It has been so good, so wonderful to get to finally know this special young woman. Does he want to ruin it because of an impulse?

I look at my husband again. He is not the same man I married. He is shaken and upset and dealing with issues I can't even begin to understand because I haven't been lied to and kept from anyone in my life. But, he has. I could make it even harder on him and tell him not to call her. But I know I won't. He's confiding in me because he doesn't want any secrets between us. He made a promise.

So I give my consent. I leave the room and give him his privacy.

Later, he describes the conversation with Sarah's mother.

Her initial response was, "I'm so sorry. I never meant to hurt anyone. I'm *so*, sorry."

She explained how she'd been engaged to another young man, Steve, but broke up with him. This is when Nick came into the picture. Within a few weeks, they became intimate, but stopped seeing each other after a few months. Then came Nick's accident. He was left with temporary amnesia. During his hospitalization, Willow went to see him, only to be turned away. Nick hadn't recognized her.

During this time, Sarah's mother found out she was pregnant. She didn't know what to do, so her first thought was to go see Nick. When Willow approached the hospital to see him, Nick's older sister, Brianna, told her to go away since she'd heard about Willow's relationship with Steve.

I suppose as a big sister, Brianna felt she had to protect Nick.

When Nick's dad saw how hurt Willow was, he snuck her into the room to see Nick. However, when Nick didn't recognize his former girlfriend, she became upset and rushed out of the hospital, distraught and heartbroken.

A few months went by, and Nick was released. When he recovered from amnesia, he saw her in town and recognized her. Her pregnant belly had started to show. She explained she was engaged to Steve. She admitted Nick had asked if the baby was his, and she'd told him it couldn't have been. She didn't explain why she lied, but at this point, she didn't know who the father was for certain.

She married, moved to Washington, and established her life there.

Nick said Willow seemed apologetic. He remained angry at her, but he told her he forgave her.

He told me he wanted to mean it when he said it.

He said she sounded relieved as they said goodbye.

*****

I don't like rollercoasters, and all these emotions reminded me of the sick feeling I get riding on one. All the ups and downs make me feel ill inside. I've never let on to anyone, especially my children. I don't want them to stress more than they are already.

Hearing about their past relationship intensifies my feelings of unease about Willow and Nick. *In a sea full of women, how could he have come to know this one so briefly? They became intimate in such a short time. Was this a case of falling hard and fast? Was it the result of teenage hormones and lack of experience on his part?*

I conclude that he responded to her because he was young and she was older and more experienced. I know people make mistakes, especially when they're young. I also know how powerful the sex drive can be—especially in teenagers.

I believe if Nick had realized his youthful indiscretion would end with this result, he might have chosen a different course. His actions show his immaturity. I know I'm nowhere near perfect myself, regardless of the way friends and family may see me. We each make what we believe is our best choice at the time and have to live with the consequences.

Nick has discovered emotions lost for countless years, and I can't blame him for wanting to know the reasons for what happened. I hope his discussion with Willow is the end of his need for closure.

*****

Sarah leaves us this morning, Monday. We say our goodbyes and hug her one last time. We watch as her car disappears around the corner.

Nick and I return to our room, and he says Willow has texted him since their phone conversation. He tells me it has changed the way he thinks about her. He asks if I want to see it.

I can tell by the look on his face this message contains another shock. I'm not sure I'm up for it. I tell him *I* don't want to read it, but I ask him to read it aloud to me.

As he reads, I know I won't be the same afterward. Fear enters my heart and takes root as he begins.

I sit on the bed and listen carefully. It's too much to process. My mind blurs events and facts into a maelstrom of data. All I hear is, "I wanted to be with you. We were meant to be together. I don't understand how it has come to this place."

She keeps saying she loved him. Loved Nick. My Nick.

Why did she send this text now? Does she hope to get him back the way they used to be? And what were they?

He's never mentioned her to me except for once, and then never by name. *And what about the accident? Was it truly an accident, or was he distraught without her?*

These thoughts cloud my mind to the point where I feel the need to escape.

Questions about his past and his feelings for this woman terrify me. *Is he telling me everything about her? Is she a threat to us, to our family? Why now? After we've welcomed Sarah into our family, why would she send such a text? She knows he's married and has children. Does she hope he still loves her and will come running back into her life with his arms wide open? Does she think he'll welcome her back like he welcomed Sarah?*

Doubt speaks to me.

By the time Nick finishes, fear shakes hands with doubt and enters the core of my being. I wonder what this woman expects of my husband, of my children, of me. *Does she know how much his family loves him? Does she realize how much we rely on him?*

Nick sees my face. He speaks in the loving way I've come to expect from him. "Sophia, I'm here with you now. I don't want her even if I might have back then. She's confused. You are my wife. I love *you*."

I look at the comforter on which we rest and begin to pick at the seams. I feel restless and worried.

"Are you okay? Do you believe me?" He appears anxious, as though my answer is important to him.

"Yes, I believe you, but now I wish you had never read her text to me. I'm nervous about her feelings. And it sounds like she still loves you, doesn't it?"

"I texted her back and told her I have a great family, a loving wife, and she needs to leave her feelings in the past. She is living in the past when she thinks of me. She has a boyfriend. I asked her to move forward and love her boyfriend, love her son, and love Sarah. It's you and me and the kids, now. I'm happy with my life. I am so blessed. I would never return to her. I even blocked her number. She can't contact me, even if she wants to."

He hugs me reassuringly. Although his words bring comfort, fear and doubt are already friends living in my heart, buried there, and delving into the "what ifs" of the situation.

The text remains on my mind and in my heart. I suspect this isn't over for Willow. Even if I've never met her, I know she still loves my husband.

CHAPTER 25 – Sarah

When I return home to Washington, I'm excited to tell everyone about my new family in California. I've talked Luke's ear off and rambled on and on about *new Dad*, the kids, Sophia, *Tia* Brianna, Grandma Alice. He couldn't keep track of who was who.

I've met with friends, my college friends, and relatives, and we've laughed and cried over how Nicholas and Sophia welcomed me into their home and their family. I've shed so many tears, but tears of joy. I'm on such a high.

The only one not happy, of course, is Mom. She and I have never been on the same page as far as my new family is concerned. She didn't support my finding *new Dad* or my siblings. Sophia's reaction was a surprise to her. Maybe she's pissed off because everything went so well. I imagine she hoped they would reject me, turn me away, and make it easier for her to get them out of the spotlight. Run back to Momma. I'm sure she'd have had her arms wide open to welcome me, her only girl. I know she didn't want to explain the whys. *Why wasn't I told? Why didn't I find out about him until the divorce? Why didn't things work out with Nicholas,* new Dad, *so many years ago?* Mom never answered these questions because I never asked her. They spun around in my head like a whirligig on a windy day.

She tries to explain one day when we're shopping, and I realize my mom never grew up or grew up so fast her life became a turbulent spinning whirlwind of events she couldn't escape. She married Steve, gave birth to me, and established a new life in Washington.

As I grew up, my features must have made Dad curious, and Mom must have suspected the real identity of my father. She knew she had been with both Nicholas and Dad at the same time. I'm sure this was hard for her to admit to me eventually since I know she loves me.

Dad may have suspected I was not his biological daughter, but he loves me the way a father would. I suspect Nicholas would have done the same had he been given the chance.

Throughout my childhood whenever I asked, Mom insisted Steve was my father. He raised me, and he deserved to be called "Dad." I love him dearly, just as he loves me. But are we in this position only because Mom moved to Washington with him to escape the fury which might have erupted if she'd told the truth?

In a small town, people can be harsh and critical. They'd have condemned her in Los Pastores or Steadfield, where everyone knew everyone else's business, and where suspicions and rumors could haunt someone until their dying day, like writing on a bathroom wall. The truth would have created problems for her and her family. But what would my life have been like if I'd known about *new Dad* and his family sooner?

I listen to Mom like the dutiful daughter I am. I respect what she's willing to share. I tell her Luke and I will get together with my new family throughout the year. I want to know my siblings, grow close to them, just like I am with Rob.

This upsets her, and we ended up parting upset, angry. I'm not sure who is more upset because I leave fast and speed away, not wanting to think about her bitter words.

I have my new family, and I will get to know them. What is so wrong with this?

To her, it must feel like the end of the world. In her mind, she's losing me to a man she's tried hard to forget. I guess it is the end of her world as she knows it.

CHAPTER 26 – Nicholas

My cell phone whistles from our headboard where I keep it. *It must be Sarah. It's evening, our time to text. Dad and daughter time.*

Sometimes this time of day, Sophia and I sit out by the pool. With the waterfall peacefully falling from the rocks, I feel tranquility settle around me. It's quiet and the kids are busy with TV or their friends.

I bring the phone outside and return her message.

It has been a few months since her visit, and now Sarah wants us to meet her husband, Luke.

She describes him as charming and interesting. A farmer at heart, he also loves the ocean. They'd like us to meet them in Santa Cruz so Luke can catch some waves. He also wants to teach the kids how to surf.

I have only spoken to Luke once since Sarah's visit. I've learned a great deal from his voice. He is calm, humorous, and interesting. His words sound natural, not practiced or planned, but like he's simply himself. I decide that I like this most about him, although I don't tell him so. I have more to learn about him. All I know for sure is he's married to my eldest daughter.

When I think about them, I feel hurt deep inside. It pains me to know I missed another major event in her life—her wedding. I wish I'd been the one to walk her down the aisle, lift her veil, kiss her softly on the cheek, and hand her over to the man she so loves. I should have shared the father-daughter dance with her as she stepped into womanhood. And I should have been the father crying as the newly married couple drove away, happily kissing through the window of their decorated limousine. *I* should have been there for her.

Sometimes in the quiet moments, which aren't many in a busy household, I remember holding Rae as a baby.

Rocking her in the La-Z-Boy. I'd marvel at what Sophia and I had created. I could watch her sleep for hours. I remember the flickering of her delicate eyelids as she slumbered, and the smiles that randomly crossed her face while baby thoughts fluttered in her mind.

Or Carissa as she'd pull herself around the house with one arm, like a desperate and thirsty traveler, dragging herself across the desert in search of an oasis. We sometimes videotaped her frustration as she tried to move forward, only to move backward in spinning circles. We used to smile at her antics. Such bittersweet memories.

I flash back to Katherine, dressed in her carefully chosen pink dress with shoes and bows to match, smiling just for me, her daddy. She's always been a diva of style and grace, even at a young age. I close my eyes reminiscing and picturing exactly what she looked like at three or four years old.

At one point, I might have taken these things for granted, but with Sarah's arrival in my life, I treasure every one. Unfortunately, I also realize I have no memories of my oldest child to hold onto. Her life was stolen from me, like a kite ripped away in a sudden gust of wind. Gone forever, never to return.

When I think too much, the pain becomes unbearable. I tell Sophia I'm overwhelmed, and she tries to comfort me. The pain dims as I recognize my blessings with her and the kids. My life is good, but I always wonder about Sarah.

What all did I miss with her? I know I'll never get those moments back.

PART II – NEW BEGINNINGS

Genevieve Galvan Frenes

CHAPTER 27 – Rae

What an awesome day. Not only do we meet Luke, but the dude takes us out surfing. I've never tried it before, so I'm psyched. Hella psyched. He makes us go through the drill first—how to lie on our bellies, paddle with our hands, feel the wave, the surge, then jump to our feet. At first I think, *Whatever. Just give me a board and let's go.*

Luke makes it look so easy. I don't care how many times I fall off. I'm surfing. We catch these ginormous waves. Okay, not so ginormous, but we still surf, and I stand up a couple of times. How cool. Now I can tell my friends I'm a surfer chick.

We practice our moves on the quietest section Luke can find. Not too many visitors, but we see all sorts of surfers—little kids, men, women, even grandpas. *Old surfer dudes on water. Man, they could break a hip or something.* I guess some people like living on the edge, even in their old age. Yeah, I can see myself like old Granddad out there, only it'll be with my boobs sagging down to my knees. What a sight.

Luke even shows us how to use his stand-up paddle board. Basically, we have to balance on this big flat board and move along with one paddle. It looks really easy, but it's hella hard. Luke looks like he's walking on water. *Wouldn't Jesus get a kick outta this?*

Billy and I go out on the board a few hundred times. Although the water is cold, I don't care. Normally, I'm crabby when I'm cold and I think to myself, *It's cold as hell out here.* But riding the SUP looks so cool. It's the awesomest thing I've done in a long time. It's something new and fun—living on the edge for once. I'm not going to miss it.

Usually, we go to the beach and watch others do cool and exciting things on the water. This time, I get to try it. Finally.

Mom and Dad aren't the crazy type, so I'm surprised when Mom lets us do it.

Katherine comes out to try the waves, too. She doesn't do too bad.

I'm surprised at how fast the day goes by. Oh, I splat on the water a lot. I feel like someone has knocked me out cold, and stupid me, I keep going back for more. *Yeah, bring it on.*

I think my new bro is all right. Kinda quiet at times. Too quiet, if you ask me. Honestly, I think he gets annoyed with my loudness. He looks at me funny sometimes, like he's thinking, "What the hell is wrong with her?" I'm used to these kinds of looks, but I don't give a rat's ass what anyone else thinks of me. I've got a new brother-in-law who surfs and stands up on water. Awesome.

CHAPTER 28 - Carissa

We spend the day at Santa Cruz with Sarah and Luke. He teaches Rae, Billy, and Katherine how to surf. Even Dad tries to get on the board. He mainly lies on his belly and paddles around. Still all right, I guess, for an old man of forty-four. Yeah, he's getting up there.

Kaden and I play in the sand, and I take pictures. I'm not too keen about smelling like seaweed or fish. Plus, I actually have to put my body into disgusting water, which who knows how many animals, plus humans, have peed in. Nasty. It's much too gross for me, so I stay with my little bro. He's my best bud, and he wants me to build sand castles with him.

Mom sits in her lounge chair and reads to her heart's content, occasionally looking up to see if anyone is drowning.

Luke seems intelligent. He takes the time to educate Rae and Billy about how to judge the waves, when to start paddling, and how not to hit the rocks. He seems a little protective of Katherine. He hasn't known her too long, but Mom and Dad are entrusting their little girl to him.

He tries to make everyone feel like they are doing well, when we really know they're not. I guess it's a sign of a good teacher and someone who knows their stuff— making kids feel comfortable and then letting them know that they can do anything. I know Dad teaches his classes this way. Yeah, my respect is already way up there for the dude, our new bro.

Sarah and I seem more comfortable talking now than we were in the beginning. I wasn't sure about her. Now, when we see each other, I don't freak out as much. Okay, well, I do a little, but not like when we first met. It still seems strange to see someone who looks so much like me.

It's sort of like those shows where someone's twin has been lost all her life. They've grown up on opposite sides of the world, and somehow, they're together again. Without warning or anything. Like *The Parent Trap*.

Suddenly, I know someone who resembles me with the same features. In a moment, we were blood and part of the same family. The worst part for me was I wasn't certain at first how it happened. Surreal, for sure.

Now, with a new brother-in-law, well, it feels like our family is expanding. We're getting older, just like them. I can't even think about turning thirty. Sarah will be twenty-seven soon. I tell her to hurry up and pop out some little pups before her vajayjay dries up. Yeah, I know it's morbid to think this way, but it's the honest truth. Once you're thirty, it all goes downhill. She can't wait forever to procreate.

As long as they don't have an entire tribe like Mom and Dad did, it'll all be good with me. One or two. I tell her (Sarah), "*Only* one or two, though. More than that, and people look at you like you're a freaking rabbit." I know, because my parents get stares.

Rae says the term "rabbit" didn't start from animals. It originated with our parents. For once, I agree with her. Still, I guess it's cool sometimes to come from a large rabbit family like ours, but *only* sometimes.

CHAPTER 29 – Katherine

Luke is a cool teacher. I never thought I could learn to ride a surfboard. Well, almost ride. I fall most of the time, but it's still neat to try. I expected to be scared of going out in the ocean because I've never tried it before, but Luke makes me feel like I can do it. So, I try surfing, and it's the greatest thing ever.

I love the feel of the waves moving me along and the freedom of being by myself in the ocean. Luke never leaves my side and keeps telling me I'm doing great. He must be an expert at this stuff because he explains step-by-step what I'm supposed to do next. No matter how many times I fall or mess up, he never laughs or makes me feel dumb. He's such as nice guy.

Luke even helps dad to get on the board, well, not to stand on the board, but he tells him how to balance with his body so he can lay on it. I'm impressed.

I can't believe I suddenly have a new brother-in-law. Not really a true brother, but close enough for me. I've decided he's part of our family forever. For Sarah and for us.

I can't imagine our lives without them—Sarah and Luke. It feels like they've always been with us. It seems so natural, like we've been together forever, but not really.

Too many years in between when we didn't know they were our family.

I'm glad I have her anyway, my new sister. She's nicer to me than Rae and Carissa sometimes. They tease me too much, and I wind up getting mad. Sarah's so sweet. She cares about what I do and say. Like when I talk to her about friends and boys. She always has good advice for me.

When I look at her, I see myself in her face. It's weird, but kinda neat, too. I've had a great day. Yeah, it's been awesome.

CHAPTER 30 – Rae

OMG. Sarah is *so* crazy. I thought I was the crazy one in the family, but she's just like me. She's loud, annoying, stylish, and hilarious all rolled up into a little midget person like me. It must be genetics. I've always felt like the odd one out, but now, well, she might just top me, not literally, of course.

We go out to eat dinner with Sarah and Luke. We all pack ourselves into a corner booth (the ones made for like ten in a family). The place is called "The Santa Cruz Café," and the owner comes out to greet us.

He's kinda stocky with a little gut on him, but very friendly. He asks where we're from, and Dad starts his story. We've heard it over and over, but we never get tired of it. How he got the email from Sarah, found her picture, knew she was his, and the rest is history.

I think it's sort of special how Sarah found us, but it does change things in our family. I'm not the oldest anymore. I now have a big sister, which I never had before. I was always the one to set the example. Now, I'm still the oldest in our family, but I have a big stepsister. OMG.

When she first came to visit us, I was so surprised. We were in Bryan's Burgers and were starving to death. I mean, I thought my stomach was eating itself, literally. We looked toward the door, and she was coming our way. This little miniature sister who, despite her age, looks like a little girl. All of us hugged her and cried. We were on a high for the rest of the night.

When we got home, she came into Carissa's room with the rest of us girls, and we talked the night away. She seemed interested in all of us and what we were involved in and like and everything. It felt so weird, like I was in a dream and had to slap myself to wake up and see if it was real. Instead, I slapped Carissa hard and got a good laugh out of the rest. LOL.

Now, with a new bro and all, I feel like we're at a new beginning, especially Dad and Sarah, but also for Luke and the rest of us. He isn't stiff or uptight. Sort of laid-back. He's annoyed with me half the time, but I couldn't care less. We're family now.

CHAPTER 31 – Carissa

My new sister has changed, altered, distorted, not quite corrupted my life (yet). I mean, when you think of your family, you tend to think of the order in which we were born. It has always been Rae, me, Katherine, and Kaden Aldana. Always, *always*, in that order.

Now, Sarah has disturbed the order of things, and well, I'm still learning to adjust my brain, the same part of my brain where I process linear patterns, and consequences, and outcomes. My brain is still analyzing Sarah's impact. My heart can catch up later.

Dad provided a brief explanation. He told us about his relationship with Willow. We found it strange to think about another woman in Dad's life. I can't picture him without my mom.

It's hard to explain Sarah to our relatives. It feels like they make up more than half of Los Pastores. On my mom's side, most are Hispanic. Each family has more than two kids, which in my mind constitutes the rabbit phenomenon, a pattern my parents obviously followed. All of the stares and the dropped jaws from cousins, *tio*s and *tia*s we've already told, were enough to send me running. Not all of Mom's family knows about Sarah. The thought of telling the rest of the clan terrifies me.

Even my dad's family's had a hard time adjusting to the news.

We went to L.A. for a family reunion. The story gradually emerged in the casual (not really casual to me) conversations at the nicely decorated table, and my dad's cousins just about hit the floor.

One of them raised his voice. "Nicholas. You of all people. Twenty-six years old. She's twenty-six. Of all people. Man."

From what I can fathom, my dad had been a momma's boy, doing no wrong at any time. All of his relatives seem to agree. He was at the heart of his family, Grandma Alice's pride and joy. After the initial shock of the story hit them, they hugged and kissed him and told him what a great guy he was for accepting his daughter.

Then all eyes turned to us. We could see them analyzing us, speculating about us. *How did they take it? How's Sophia doing?* Like we were slabs of meat hanging in a meat locker, just sides of beef to be poked and prodded by the foreman. I felt like they were getting ready to chop us up. I expected them to question the hell out of us then spit us out.

We didn't do anything. He did.

Trying to explain the situation to the rest of the world is even more difficult.

*****

I have an assignment in my Spanish class to create a family tree.

Really? Now? Couldn't it be something simple like my favorite food or favorite TV show? Mi comida favorita es... This would have been much simpler.

Instead, the other students look at my family tree and ask, "*¿Quién es esta hermana?* Who is this sister?" Or they ask, "Why do you have so many sisters? *¿Por qué tiene tantas hermanas?*"

My mind flashes to a cage filled with a million zillion rabbits, multiplying by the second, with the mama and papa rabbits bearing my parents' names.

"*No sé.* I don't know. Sarah is my *el half sistero.*" So, yeah, my Spanish sucks because my mom and dad white washed their children. Mom swears she tried to teach us Spanish when we were little, but she got tired of our whining and whimpering. Now, I wish I could communicate better. Mom knows how to speak Spanish, but we still don't.

So, our family story has definitely changed my view of us. I mean, when I hear different stories about my dad, I have to rethink my original feelings about him. I'm not resentful, just observant. *Who are you now?*

I ask myself what I thought about him before. He's always acted like a nice guy, maybe a little too talkative for me, especially in the mornings when my brain doesn't start working until after the coffee hits my nerves. Then again, I'm the quiet one. He's definitely a hard worker, but wants to work non-stop twenty-four/seven and wants us to do the same.

I'm not a child workaholic wannabe—too much effort required.

As for emotion, he's always been more emotional than Mom. I guess most mothers tend to have more mood swings, but Dad has random OCD moods. He gets teary eyed when he thinks of Grandpa Alfred. Something sentimental comes on TV, and he breaks down.

There's also the faithful Catholic part of him. He constantly tells us to attend Mass and stay close to God.

This is how I thought of him before Sarah came.

I still think the same about dear old Dad. I can't envision him without my mom. It's hard to think of him with another woman. Even the thought feels disloyal. My parents are like the poster couple for the eternal Catholic marriage.

They still spend time together, go on dates, still check with each other about decisions, especially with ones concerning us kids, and they have maybe one fight per year. The lovey-dovey nonsense we experience in our household gets to be too much sometimes. Honestly, I have to walk out of the room. But then again, most of my friends' parents are divorced, separated, or in the process of divorce. So I guess I can tolerate the lovey-dovey stuff. My parents' marriage seems like a rare gem archaeologists uncover in a dig.

When we found out about Sarah, I was afraid the gem was going to shatter. I mean like earth-shattering, but in a miracle from God, it didn't.

Mom is a stickler for rules and conduct. Always wants and expects the best of people. When she doesn't get this treatment, she lets everyone know. The whole house hears about it. Honestly, the house sometimes rattles from her expectations.

I imagine she had to bite the bullet on this one, and do the Catholic thing by standing by Dad. It sort of surprised me when she didn't blow up or leave for a few days or anything after she found out about Sarah. I mean, I expected her to be gone, and honestly, I would have understood.

I don't know if I could have been as strong. Mom spends a lot of time locked away in her room, not sharing or talking to any of us about how she feels. She's really quiet and private about what she's going through. It's hard to tell if she's hurting. I'm a lot like her. Neither of us shows our pain. It has helped to have a strong parent to support us while we've tried to cope.

Despite the rabbit jokes and questions from people in our lives, I still like my family, even the new midget, Sarah. I can't blame Dad for bringing Sarah into our family because he's doing the logical thing any good guy would do—owning up to his responsibilities and being a man of God.

Now, Dad's discussions about premarital sex have changed from the impact of an earthquake to the tremble of an aftershock. He can't say much anymore.

Now he can tell us, *"Do as I say, not as I do,"* because he did. We learn better from actions. In this case, Dad is using his experience to show us what *not* to do when we're stupid and horny. This describes nearly every teenager on earth.

I respect him even more now.

Like Mom said, "One moment a million years ago doesn't define how a person is today." My dad sure isn't the same ignorant boy he was at nineteen.

Despite my annoyance in him at times, he has a good heart and wants the best for us kids.

CHAPTER 32 – Kaden

Today I played with my LEGOs for a long, long time, ate a peanut butter and jelly sandwich and drank milk, and then played outside with Ricky and Danny, my buddies. They are my neighbors. Danny and me are six, and Ricky is seven. We've been buddies since we moved in.

Then after I came inside, we ate dinner, took a shower, and now, I have to go to sleep. I hate going to bed. I lie down and my eyes blink and blink. It takes forever to fall asleep. All I want to do is play.

Tonight, I asked Mommy about Sarah. "Where did she come from? Who brought her to us? How come she's so old?"

I don't remember if Mommy answered my questions because then she asked me what I thought of my new sister.

I told her, "I like Sarah, and she's nice to me. She helped me get dressed one day. It was weird because I didn't really know her, but it felt nice, like when you help me get ready for school. She seems older, like you, Mommy, but she plays with me like my other sistas. She's into silly, funny stuff."

I told her I liked our day at the beach. I liked how the sand went through my fingers and how when I walk on the sand, it goes between my toes. I liked building sand castles with Carissa and watching the others try to surf. Sista and I laughed every time Rae and Billy hit the water. It looked like it hurt, but they kept going back in. The water looked scary. It was so cold I didn't want to get wet or try surfing.

Anyway, tonight Mommy and I said prayers together. I said a prayer for Sarah.

I know Sarah is my sista, but I don't understand something. Mommy and Daddy had Rae, Carissa, Katherine, and me. I've seen baby pictures of my sistas, but not Sarah. Where has Sarah been all of this time? Mommy didn't have her, so who did? There are no pictures of her when she was little. I've seen lots and lots of pictures of us, especially when we were babies. We have books and books of pictures. I don't see any for Sarah.

When I ask questions, Mommy just says Sarah's my sista and I should love her like my other sistas. She says one day she'll explain all about Sarah, and then I'll understand.

Sometimes I wish I was big so I could understand like everyone else. I know something isn't right, but I don't know what it is.

CHAPTER 33 – Katherine

I text Sarah all the time.

"Sarah, you up?" I text in the dark. It's past midnight and I can't sleep.

"Hey, sis, what you up to? How's school? Friends?" Sarah texts back.

"Everything is good. Sorry it's late. I couldn't sleep and well, I thought I'd just see if you were up, too."

"No problem, little sis. I hope you're doing okay."

"I miss you, Sarah. Wish you lived close by so we could hang out."

"Oh, I miss you too. We'll have to get together again soon."

When I first saw Sarah, I wanted to cry. It seemed crazy for this to be happening to our family.

When Mom told us Dad wanted to see us in his room, I felt my heart race because I didn't know what was happening. After he told us the whole story, I was the first one to start crying. I didn't even know why. My tears kept falling no matter how fast I tried to wipe them away. It was like too much stuff to think about at one time. My brain was like on fire from too much information, and my emotions were like a rollercoaster, up and down, terrified and then relieved the next minute.

After we heard the whole story, my sisters and I felt a little awkward like, "Now what?" Once we found out Mom was okay with everything, my sisters and I were excited to meet another sister. I talked to Sarah on the phone soon after, and we've been close ever since.

It all happened in a blink. Well, actually not that fast, but within a month, she came to see us.

While she was here, we looked through old albums, the ones Mom made for each of us when we were little. When Sarah saw my pictures, she said, "You look just like me at that age. We look so much alike here. See?" She would point out each picture to me. When I saw her face, I wanted to cry again. She never got to be part of our family, I mean the one with Mom, Dad, my sisters, and Kaden, and me.

Where was she then? Does she ever wonder about what she missed when she wasn't here? Does she ever think about times like birthdays and celebrations with our family and feel bad?

I mean, Mom and Dad have always tried to make our lives fun. Like the time they surprised all of us and took us to the Gwen Stefani concert, on a school night, even.

Sometimes we go to the beach and eat at our favorite fish restaurant, Gil's Fish Market, in Monte del Oro. The Aldana crew barely fits on one table and we have to scrunch together on the small benches. We warm each other up when the cold wind makes us freeze, and we shoo away the seagulls when they try to get our chicken tenders and fish. Dad and Mom eat their favorite fish, and my sisters and brother and I eat chicken tenders.

We went to the California Mid-State Fair in Los Palos. We ate to our hearts' content and rode on everything. They let us stay up super-duper late to ride the cool rides because it was too hot during the day. We wound up by nighttime.

I think about the concerts, like Eric Church and Maroon 5, Rae, Carissa, and I saw because Mom and Dad let us go. We went by ourselves, when we got a little older. They waited outside or went to eat dinner, then came back for us at the gate. Of course, we knew they'd never leave us.

Yeah, our parents have always tried to give us fun memories, and we appreciate it, but Sarah wasn't with us.

I feel sad, even guilty, when I think about what Sarah missed. I wonder why her parents kept her away from us. She could have been part of our family all along. I want to cry just thinking about it.

Then, I think about everything Dad's told us about Sarah's mom. I feel bad for Mom. She has to hear about this now—after having all of us kids.

Now, Sarah is here. And somehow, Mom is able to love her. I really don't understand how she can, but it must be an adult thing.

I love my mom for loving Sarah. I want to hug her to death for letting Sarah be part of our family. I'm sure a lot of wives would be angry at their husbands. Some women might even leave their husbands for something like this, but not my mom. Mom tries to keep her head on straight, even when with issues like this. I don't know if I could react like she has, but I'm glad because now we have Sarah with us forever.

Sarah wants us to get together again soon. Our weekend visit with her at the beach was a blast. I wish we could see her more often, but I guess Luke can't take time off from work since he's a farmer. Sarah says he works hard. Washington is a long way from us, but now we're family. I hope we can stay with her and see their farm. She says maybe after school is out. I can't wait.

CHAPTER 34 – Rae

So, when I think about everything in our life now, I'm like, *WTF?*

I'm the life of the party with my gift of smart aleck personality (the queen of bullcrap herself), and don't seem like I could ever be down, but there are times when my life is like hella ironic. Yeah, that's the word—ironic.

I mean, all of Dad's preaching to us girls about waiting until marriage, no premarital sex, no boyfriends until we were fifteen. The list went on and on about how we were supposed to act according to the house rules of conduct. All of this protective crap.

Really, Dad?

We heard about this forever from you. And then, here comes Sarah out of the blue, like some damn spaceship landing out of the effing sky. Sometimes *I* feel like the alien in this hella weird family. Sometimes it feels like I'm stuck on some planet by myself since our world turned upside down.

Okay, the first initial shock about Sarah was enough to make me pee in my pants. When Dad called us into the room, I thought for sure we were in for it. His serious face and nervous look made me want to hide. I was sure we had done something wrong and didn't even know it. That's what I thought at first.

Then, he started to tell us what was going on—about Willow, then about Sarah. I thought I was in some kind of bizarre dream.

But then, I saw my dad's face, so tired and beaten down, and well, I felt sorry for the dude. I mean, Dad has always tried to lead us down the right path, take us to Mass, watch who we hang out with. All the stuff concerned dads do for their kids, especially their daughters. He treated us like delicate flowers, who needed to be protected from the evil forces of shit out in La-La Land.

Part of me wants to cheer at his attempt to act like a dad. *Yea, dad.* So many of my friends don't even know who their fathers are, and the ones who do aren't in the picture. Some of my friends have never met their dads.

My dad told us all about his past no-nos and about this woman, Willow. I always thought it had just been him and Mom. Dad never mentioned anyone else in his life before her.

After he finished telling us about Sarah, I figured it took a lot of balls to tell all three of us about another daughter. What else could we do but love him and accept Sarah, just like Mom did?

I wasn't pissed at the time, but afterward, I felt, well, confused.

I felt stuck in a sea of stormy water and was slowly drowning, trying to hold onto rocks, but really, they weren't real rocks. They were sort of like Styrofoam. The more I reached for them, the more I bobbed, grasping for something to hold me up. It's taken about six months for me to understand how our lives have changed.

TBH, it scared the shit out of me when Sarah showed up at Bryan's Burgers, the first time. I mean, we got a call from Sarah a month before. Then, bam. Suddenly, she drops into our laps like some long lost puppy wandering for twenty-six years. Hella weird and hella too soon for me. I don't know about Carissa and Katherine, but if I was old enough, I'd have downed a few cold ones to help get through it.

I didn't realize how screwed up my mind and heart were until later on.

Don't get me wrong, I love Sarah and everything about her shrimpy little self. She's definitely an Aldana. But damn, it's too much. I never say anything to Dad or Mom, though. I don't want them to feel bad. It's been tough for both of them. Honestly, I thought they were on a diet or something because they lost so much weight, and neither of them ate like their old selves. This was before we knew

Sarah was coming. I guess they were as nervous about meeting her as we were.

Oh, and Mom with her freaking OCD cleaning. OMG. She went crazy. In those weeks before Sarah's surprise visit, I couldn't put a stinking cup down before she had it picked up, washed, dried, and put away. She found all of my candy stashes in the cushions of the couch upstairs and threw them away. Threw them away. That was some beautiful sugar.

And she cleaned my room. She's always implied, never yelled or fussed too much, my room's a danger zone, but she actually went in and tackled the heap. Gathered up and stashed all of my dirty (and possibly clean) clothes. I mean, even *I* couldn't see the floor when I went into my room, my comfortable room. I had to smell the clothes to see it they were clean or not. Yeah, I knew something was up when she was brave enough to take it on. My beautiful paradise.

Well, no surprise to anyone, Dad doesn't bring up the premarital sex thing anymore. He tells us he wants us to make better choices than he made. We nod and listen like good, obedient children. What else can we do?

The preaching has gone away, like a dripping faucet with a new washer. Why would he ever bring it up again? I mean, *really.*

All of us—Carissa, Katherine, and I—think the same thing.

Yeah right, Dad. Sure.

My sisters and I look at Sarah's picture on the living room wall. *Yep, Dad, you don't have to say anything more.*

PART III - WASHINGTON

CHAPTER 35 – Nicholas

I pack the car. Mom arrives and I load her things. Thank God the girls didn't bring every piece of clothing they own. Boys are easier. A pair of jeans, a t-shirt, and a broken in Dodger hat. So much easier.

We leave around midnight.

Sophia can't wait to get going. Even though the trip will be a long one, she's ready to get on the road. We've agreed to split the driving so that we can make it in one trip.

We're burnt out from school. I know she's nervous about meeting Sarah's family. She's hasn't talked to me about this aspect of the visit, but I sense her anxiety. I can't blame her.

I'm anxious to see the Williamson farm, filled with apple trees and acres of wheat. I'm curious about Luke's equipment. Sarah talks about the huge machines his crew uses to harvest their crops. I can't envision these gigantic pieces of equipment, but then again, I'm not a farmer. Even living here in the Chia Valley, with many farms surrounding us, I wouldn't know which machine is used for what purpose. It seems complicated, but I know I'll be able to figure it out after Luke shows me. Gadgets intrigue me.

He's told me about a new seed he and his uncle produce and sell now. Some form of cost-effective wheat. He seems wise for his age, a good match for Sarah. Level-headed too. Not a showoff. I like this most about him. He's just himself.

It will be a long drive through California and Oregon to Washington. Sarah and Luke live in the small town of Cloverston. Their farm is huge, but the town itself appears small and quaint. I looked it up on the Internet. One elementary school. A small market. A tiny post office.

I like small towns. They remind me of the country in the vicinity of Los Pastores where we live. I grew up in Los Angeles and appreciate the stillness and peace I've found in this rural area.

I'm curious and nervous about what will happen when we meet Sarah's family.

CHAPTER 36 – Sophia

We're on our way. The car is packed to the max, and the kids are content with their iPods plugged in their ears with their music blasting. Typical teenagers. I can hear some of their racket, even though they each wear ear buds, but as long as they're quiet, I'm fine.

My mother-in-law, Alice, is with us. She seems excited to be going somewhere out-of-state and meeting Sarah's husband, Luke.

As the sun comes up, the scenery passes before me like pictures on my phone—landscapes, water, trees, and rolling hills, I observe quickly and then they're gone in a flash.

We can definitely tell when we arrive in Washington. We inhale and appreciate the clean air, rare in California. It has grown fresher as we've traveled north through Oregon. Now here in Washington, we breathe easily.

Minutes turn to hours in anticipation of the moment when we'll finally arrive in Cloverston.

As we are approach the town, I send Sarah a text. Normally, her excited, bubbly personality comes across through her texts, but this time seems different.

"We're almost there. I'm excited," I text.

I wait for her reply. She responds a few minutes later. "Okay, when you get close, call me for directions."

I try to shrug off her brusque tone. I wonder if her invitation was only a polite invite, the kind people issue automatically but really don't mean. The excitement of the moment leads them to blurt it out loud, only to regret their words later. *Is this what's happened?*

I turn to Nick. "Did Sarah talk to you about our coming to see her?"

"What do you mean?"

"Well, did she feel okay about our visit? Did you sense any anxiety or anything?"

"She didn't say much. Why?"

"Just wondering." The churning in my stomach is a sign I know well. It's my gut instinct about something not quite right. I try to ignore it, but it doesn't go away. I've felt it before, as if it's a warning about something bad to come. I try to shoo it away, like a fly pestering me on a hot, muggy day. But my apprehension remains.

At dusk, we seem lost and follow the GPS directions on our phones. The girls are more skilled at this task than I am, and I find myself looking at a red moving button on a phone. It makes no sense to my brain.

Near nightfall, we finally arrive in Cloverston. As I'd expected, it's a quaint town, about one street long, with a small market, kids on bikes, and lots of fields surrounding the town. The Cashup wheat waves to us as the wind from the car pushes the strands along like an undulating rhythm set to music of its own. The beauty of the fields, like a drawing in a gallery, shows God's rich creation. I am filled with wonder. Clean air, beautiful flowers, trees, and more Cashup surrounds us.

At last, I spot the sign, "Williamson Farm." We've arrived.

A long, paved driveway lined with Red Alder trees finally leads us to their house. Luke and Sarah walk out of the door. They are holding hands. She looks tense and worried. I wonder if she is really okay with us being here. I don't say a word to Nick about my concerns, of course, because he's beaming. Alice finally gets to meet our new son-in-law.

"Grandma," Sarah exclaims loudly as she sees Alice get out of the van. Everyone gives her big hugs and lots of kisses. The kids can't wait to get out and stretch. They put on their sweaters as the cool Washington weather is unfamiliar to us. It's July and we're not accustomed to cold.

Luke takes us on a quick tour of the place, and we see his equipment. It's enormous, varied, and looks expensive. He is definitely happy as a farmer, made to live on the land. He obviously takes pride in his work. The kids love it here.

Their home is an older '70s split-level, remodeled by Luke's uncles for them when they moved in. It is dark brown on the outside. A large patio extends along the back of the house. Inside, the living room has a grand piano with a sitting area. Nearby is the kitchen, with a large oak table. The kitchen extends into a sitting area. The full basement holds three rooms, plus the laundry room and exercise room. We decide to bunk downstairs with Alice.

The girls take the upstairs rooms Sarah has decorated specifically for them. Rae's has flowing curtains with a white four-poster bed. It befits our diva. The simple décor, with a bit of flash is right up Rae's alley.

Carissa's room is purple (her favorite color) with a comfy bed and simple decorations. She likes her room instantly. Katherine's room is downstairs where we'll sleep. Very simple and tasteful, her room has blue tones, with lace on the bedspread, perfect for Kat and her sense of fashion. Kaden decides he will sleep with his closest sister in the purple room.

Sarah and Luke are prepared for us, and s'mores are our treat for the night. The kids jump with excitement and encircle the fire pit where the s'mores will be made.

Since the night air is cool, we cover ourselves with blankets. Laughing voices fill the air, and the night takes on a dreamlike quality where I sit and wonder. *How did we get to this point?* I look at the kids' faces, including Sarah's. *How did God bring us together from two different worlds miles apart? The kids, Sarah and Luke, us— somehow we all fit together. This is our family.*

Eventually, warmth calls us back inside and welcomes us with comfy blankets and soft pillows. I hug my pillow, close my eyes, and melt into the silent night.

CHAPTER 37 – Sarah

I'm not ready. I'm just not ready for them to be here. I know I invited them, and I've missed them, but now, I don't know what to do, how to act. Who am I when I'm with them? We haven't known each other long. I meant it when I asked them to come. I thought we'd be okay, but now I'm not so sure.

There's also the Hispanic thing. In Washington, practically every Latino person is a field worker. Growing up here, it never dawned on me there was anything wrong with Spanish-speaking people working on the land around us. This has been a daily sight most of my life. Now, here's my new family, Hispanic, educated, lovely people. *Will my friends and Luke's family accept them?* I can picture their expressions when they take a look at the girls and me. I have always known I had some other ethnicity, but now here's living proof. *Will everyone treat me differently? Will they hurt my family's feelings?*

And what about Mom and Dad? I wanted them here, but Luke practically called me a moron for even considering the idea. Really? *After all of these years, can* new Dad *learn to love them? Can he see how happy I am and how loved I was despite his not being in the picture?*

Luke says it's not a good idea. "Nicholas is a good guy, but he may not see things the way you do."

A terrible feeling has been gnawing at me. Guilt. Guilty about not loving Mom and Dad enough. Not having them here to meet my new family. Guilty about not accepting my new family wholeheartedly. Guilt has been stomping me down this week. I'm trampled and worn out, and they just arrived. I don't know how long I'll hold up.

Luke has been supportive. He gave me a pep talk before they got here, telling me everything will work out, saying everyone will love my new family, telling me they'll fit in here. I listen to him, but my nerves rattle, and I ache just thinking about all the possibilities.

Mom texts about how much she loves me, how they (Mom and Dad and Rob) are my real family. "Yes, they look like you, but they aren't like you."

In a way, she's right, but I don't want to agree. She kept me away from him, and now I have to figure all this out by myself.

I just want to go out on the pond in the floaties and not have to think about any of this. Float and stop thinking all of these painful thoughts—push them away and drift away to some other land.

I love them all so much, but I feel like a thousand hands are pulling me in opposite directions, and I'm being shredded to pieces.

CHAPTER 38 – Nicholas

What a perfect day. It's Sunday, and it's early. The rest of the clan is asleep so I head off to church. After attending Mass at a Catholic church nearby, I come home to find Mom and Sarah at the kitchen table, drinking coffee. About half an hour later, Sophia comes upstairs and hugs Sarah from behind. "Good morning."

"Hey, Sophia. I don't know what you guys want to eat." I respond. "Oh, cereal or toast will be fine. Just let me know where things are, and I'll make it."

She points out where the coffee and cereal are located. Mom volunteers to help. I had called Sarah before to see what to bring, but she said she had it covered.

Soon, Sarah's friend, Heather shows up. I think it's a bit odd for her friend to come over so early on a weekend, but I don't let on because I don't know her routine.

Sarah and Heather leave to get groceries for a barbeque. Again, we offer to help them with the cost of items, but they say it is okay. We clean up the kitchen after they leave.

Luke tells us his family is coming along with Sarah's brother, Rob, and her longtime friend-sisters, as she calls them, Heather and Amber.

I imagine it must be a little weird for Rob to grow up thinking Sarah was his completely biological sister, only to discover they were only half related. I hope he'll be cool about everything, but then there are his parents. *Will he report back to them? Fill them in on Sarah's other family?* I don't care what they think of me, but I'm protective of Sophia and the kids. I can't imagine what her parents think about them.

Her parents? My mind races.

Honestly, to hell with what they think. Here I go again—the rant starts in my head whenever I think of anything associated with having missed all of Sarah's early years.

I want to blow up every time I think about the two of them and what they knew. What honest human beings would keep the truth from their only daughter? I don't know how they lived with themselves all those years. *Are they in pain because now I'm here in her world?* I'm sorry to say, I'm glad if they are.

Now Sophia and my family know the truth, and my anger diminishes. Sophia is able to see things from all perspectives. I envy her ability to be rational.

I can't always see both sides of an issue. In this instance, my anger still sometimes gets the best of me, eats at me, and drives me crazy. Maybe it's because they knew the truth and chose to keep someone so precious away from me for so long. *How do they justify it?* Until my dying day, I will never understand what made them act the way they did.

As for God, well He can forgive anyone. Even people who'd do this to a little girl. But I'm not ready to nor will I be ready for a long time. I know I told Willow I forgave her, but the pain of their act will stay with me always. I can't seem to let it go.

I remind myself I'm in Sarah's world right now. She's been hurt enough, and I don't want her to know my feelings.

My thoughts are quiet and private. They scatter my mind in a billion pieces, even when everything appears normal. They cloud my thinking and turn my usually calm, laid-back persona into a distraught and broken man I know I wasn't meant to be. For Sarah, I'll say nothing and pray I can keep it together on this trip. Pray a lot.

CHAPTER 39 – Sophia

I've been most anxious about this day in particular ever since we knew we were coming. Sarah's brother will be here and so will Luke's relatives. I struggle with how to dress since it's warm outside, and I don't know what others will be wearing. My anxiety increases as the day wears on. Two o'clock finally arrives. Time for the party to begin.

The guests begin to arrive. Close friends, family members, college buddies—their names become a blur as we smile and shake hands, hoping our first impressions are good ones. Luke puts chicken on the grill as Sarah prepares other side dishes to take onto the porch. We offer to help, but they say they have things under control.

Sarah's close friend, Amber, introduces herself to me. She seems shy, so I may get along with her since I'm not the life of the party myself. She tells me her mother was a close friend of Willow's and she's known Sarah since they were babies.

She looks at Sarah's sisters, my girls, and shakes her head. "I always knew something wasn't quite right. When we were kids, Sarah didn't look anything like her brother, or her dad. She did resemble her mom in some ways, mostly her mannerisms. I always wondered. I think my mom did, too, but she never asked. Now, seeing your daughters, I'm amazed at how much Sarah looks like them. I just can't get over the resemblance."

"Well, I guess, you'd know better than I would. When I first saw Sarah's picture, I knew she was Nick's. No one could mistake the similarities. I'm glad he's connected to her."

"It's just so great she found him and for all of you to accept her into your family. I'm so glad you came." Amber smiles.

"I am, too." I return her smile.

The guests sit on the beautiful lush grass in the backyard and begin to eat. I'm reminded of a museum painting where smiling faces, pleasant in conversation, seem etched on the canvas. The colorful palette of surrounding colors of grass and trees and flowers adds to the ambiance. Mothers and fathers sit beside their small children. They all enjoy their meals and laugh throughout the afternoon.

I spot my girls, the only dark-haired beings amid the guests. They grab seats on a bench around the apple tree, the one Luke built for Sarah when they first got married. My little Kaden sits closest to Carissa. Luke told us the story during our orientation walk around the property.

The tree is a bit apart from the rest of the crowd, yet my kids can still see what is happening. I take my plate to join them. Nearby, some of Sarah's friends sit on the grass and talk with her.

As the day wears on, Luke and his friends begin to play a game with two sticks and a Frisbee. We discover this game is called Beer Frisbee. It's played by placing an empty beer bottle on the top of each pole. Each player's job is to knock the beer bottle off of the top of their opponent's stick with the Frisbee. The poles are thirty to forty feet apart. I surmised this is a college game since beer is involved and Luke plays with some of his buddies from Washington State. The game seems silly at first, but as the crowd dies down, we become more intrigued. Those of us who remain gather around to watch.

Kaden, noting the Frisbee and the sticks, asks for a description of the game. Luke encourages him to give it a try. Kaden's opponent is Sarah's brother, Rob. They go back and forth. The Frisbee and the empty beer bottles near collapse give us all a laugh.

As the sun goes down and the cool air sets in, I contemplate Sarah's two brothers, Rob and Kaden. They shake hands at the end of a round, a twenty-something-year-old and a six-year-old. *Is this really happening?*

Generations apart and worlds apart, they've found something else in common besides their sister.

As the cleanup begins, we head inside to help Sarah in the kitchen. Soon, an older, striking lady comes into the dining room. Luke introduces us to his mother, Mina. She smiles, shakes our hands, and hugs Nick.

"I've heard the entire story. I just love Sarah, and the way you responded to her, well, it's just beautiful. What a blessing this is, just miraculous. I'm so glad you found each other."

"I am, too." Nick smiles.

"I brought some wine. We should all have a toast." She opens the bottle and pours some into our glasses. I notice her beautiful and flawless skin. In the soft light, she resembles a much younger woman. I'm also intrigued by her spirit.

"To Sarah and Nicholas and all of you." She raises her glass. "Cheers."

Of course we respond and clink our glasses.

As we lie in bed that evening, we agree we're in awe of what has taken place.

Nick turns toward me. "So what do you think?"

"I thought things went well. Didn't you? I was nervous at first, but everyone was very nice. What did you think of Rob? Of Luke's mom?"

"Rob seems like a good guy. Look at the way he played with Kaden. He treated the kid as an equal. I admired him for doing it. He seems cool. I'm sure Kaden would agree."

I share his opinion.

"Luke's mom is very nice. I wish she'd arrived earlier. Luke's dad didn't come with her. What do you think that was all about?"

"I don't know, but I did notice everyone else was here except him. Maybe he's just not a people person, or doesn't like crowds, or doesn't like meeting new people. I don't know, but Luke sure is a nice guy. Overall, I think everything turned out just right." I snuggle against my husband.

"Me, too. What a great day."

Nicholas kisses me goodnight. We close our eyes to the flawless day and dream of more to come.

CHAPTER 40 – Sarah

I'm so glad it's over with. The stares and the comments from everyone. It was almost too much to bear. Everyone kept looking at them then back at me, especially my close friends. They told me they never expected the others to look like me. *If they knew something was up all these years, why didn't they say anything to me?* Now I know for sure what all the whispers and looks were about. This is too much and too soon. I never should have invited my new family to come here. Now, there's no going back.

Luke says I'm overreacting. Everything went well, and everyone got along just fine. "What's the big deal?" he asks.

The big deal is I now have two families. When I look at them, one is white and fair-skinned, and the other is Mexican and brown-haired. Here in Washington, this combination isn't necessarily a good thing. I don't know what Luke's family thinks since all of their hired hands look like my new family. Nor do I know what my new family thinks of all of my blonde, blue-eyed friends and relatives. I want to run away and hide, but I can't.

I definitely can't run back to Mom and Dad. What will they say? *Maybe, you should have left things alone, and not gone searching for your father or this new family connected to some other world. We said you weren't going to like what you found. Now what?*

This weekend when they arrived, Mom and Dad texted to check on me, just like I'm still a little girl. "How are you doing?" "How is it with all of them in the house with you?" I feel like I can't breathe.

I decide to invite Heather over again. I tell her it would be fun to head to the pond and float around in the sun. Heather is always there for me, so I know she's in.

The rest of the family says it sounds good, but when we look in the garage, we find only three floaties.

Oh well, they'll figure it out.

I've got to get to the pond with Heather and Rae. Grandma Alice and Kat say they'll come with us. Sophia and *new Dad* are going to get more floaties. I give them quick directions, so they should find the place fine. I'm too exhausted to care about anything else.

CHAPTER 41 – Nicholas

I'm so pissed. I come with my family all the way from California to see my eldest daughter, and she treats me like I'm nobody.

I'm just coming off of yesterday's high when Sophia tells me we're going to the pond. Sarah, Heather, and Rae go on ahead. Since there aren't enough floaties, we'll have to go get some from the store. This irritates me a bit, but I don't let on. *Just go with the flow.*

We get to the store and look around for water gear. It's getting close to noon, and I ask about lunch.

Sophia says she doesn't think Sarah has plans since she didn't mention it. "Why would she be concerned about us? She's used to her life consisting of her and Luke. She doesn't have kids. Heck, she still hangs out with her college friends. She lives in a different world, babe."

Why would she give any thought to our needs? Because, maybe it would show she loved us enough to think ahead and consider us and our feelings.

I shake my head and go to the register to pay for the floaties and some groceries. Although I'm half Caucasian, the Hispanic part of me can see our cultures are just not the same. When relatives visit, they are treated with importance. At this point, I don't feel very special.

As we follow directions to the pond, it's as though we're traveling in a foreign country. The road on the map, which is supposed to veer to the right doesn't exist, so we turn around and head the other way, only to become more confused. I start to fume. *Why would she think we could find this place out in the sticks?*

After another hour trying to find the pond, we head back to the house. They still aren't home, and we're famished.

Sophia unloads the groceries and makes sandwiches.

I'm mad, and the smell of food doesn't make things better. I feel like my head might pop off my shoulders. Without eating, I go downstairs and try to sleep. Sleep never comes nor does my anger subside.

After about half an hour, I hear voices as people arrive. I stay downstairs, afraid of the words waiting to spew from my mouth. They might make the windows shatter.

After a few minutes, Sophia walks into the room.

I lie on the bed and stare into the calm eyes of reason.

"So what did she say?" I ask.

"She was hungry and made herself a sandwich. When she asked where we'd been, I told her it took some time to get the floaties. Then lunchtime was near, so we bought some food. I said the directions were a bit confusing, and we got lost. She looked defensive. She didn't apologize, but said she explained carefully, and it was easy to find. I just told her we misunderstood, not a big deal."

"Don't you think she was rude to leave us to do all of this by ourselves?"

Sophia shrugs and sits on the edge of the bed. "I don't know. Maybe, but she doesn't think like us, babe. She may be twenty-six years old, but she still lives in the world of college friends and is used to having this big old house to herself. I don't think she meant to hurt you. She's just being herself and thinks nothing of it. She seemed defensive, but I didn't start anything. We don't know her well yet."

I don't know how she does it, this woman, my wife. She understands as if blessed with the grace of God. She has such insight, and I wish I had as much. But I'm still pissed. I want her to be flipping mad along with me, but it isn't going to happen.

Sophia brushes an unruly lock of hair off my forehead. "Do you want to eat now?"

I turn around and try to fall asleep. Anger isn't a good roommate.

*****

Sarah wants to talk. I haven't seen her since yesterday. I tried to find her in her bedroom last night, but something went wrong. Now we sit outside on the back patio.

She turns on me with her eyes blazing. "Nicholas, I don't know what's happened. Our awkwardness, your pissed off mood, or whatever is it. I shouldn't feel like this in my own house." She taps one hand into the other with each point, like she's chopping her way through her own anger.

"I didn't mean to startle you. I just wanted to talk." *My daughters would never speak to me like this, never.*

"Well, *Nicholas*, no man is allowed to enter my bedroom except for my husband. You scared me. Really scared me. Even my brother never goes in there. There's a proper way of doing things. You spooked me."

Spooked you? Why would you use the word "spooked"? Like I slithered into your room. What am I, a snake? What about a molester? You don't use these words, but I'm sure they're just waiting to jump off of your tongue.

"I'm sorry, I just wanted to talk. When my girls have problems, I walk into their rooms. I was trying to find you alone, away from the others. I need to figure out how things got so mixed up—first the pond incident and now this misunderstanding." I can see by her stern expression she doesn't accept what I'm saying.

"Well, *Nicholas*, my parents raised me to expect a right to my privacy. This is not how we handle things. What were you were trying to accomplish with your quiet anger? I just don't get it. We yell. We scream if we have to. We get it all out, and then we move on. That's how it works in *my* family."

"*Your parents*? I should have been one of the people who raised you. Your parents didn't tell you everything, did they? Your so-called dad? He had to have known. Look at you. You mean to tell me that every damn day he looked in the mirror and didn't wonder why you didn't look remotely like him? You look just like me. They kept you from me."

"My parents love me. Even my dad, he loves me the best way he can. He's always been there for me and loves me like his daughter." She turns her eyes directly on mine.

"Don't you love me? I'm your *real* father, not him."

She sets her jaw. "Nicholas, I like you a lot, but we need more time to get to know each other. I'm sure I could love you."

I feel daggers tear into my heart with each word from her mouth.

"So that's it. You could've been with us all these years. They did this to you, to me. All these damn years. They knew all along, and they didn't say a thing to you. *They* kept *you* from *me*." My voice shakes as I slam my hand on the patio table.

Her body jolts. She shakes her head, not acknowledging or caring about anything I've said. I know she'll never understand. The truth will never come out, and the truth needs to be told. Ironically, this deception is the only thing we have in common—the knowledge of Sarah as a missing piece in my life. They pretended Steve was her dad, but Willow must have seen me in Sarah's face. Seen it from day one and kept it from all of us.

"I'm done with this."

With that, I slam the door, not caring if I break it. It doesn't break, thank God, but with each step I take, I hear my heart thunder in my ears. My eyes flood with tears.

My dark shades hide the truth, except from Sophia. Her calm face greets me, and in an instant, she knows. It is done.

CHAPTER 42 – Sarah

Heather comes to the house when I call her after the blowup. The sight of her maroon GMC truck in the driveway is a relief.

She shakes her head. "The nerve of him, scaring you like that. What a jerk." She scowls.

"He just won't listen. He just doesn't get how creeped out I got when he came into my room. Why couldn't he have knocked or called out to me? I would have come out to talk to him. He scared the *hell* out of me."

My fear had surprised me. His face wasn't familiar in the dim light. It took me by surprise. The anxiety, the fear, came to me with a pounding heart and sweaty palms. I wanted to run out of the room, past the figure in the dark. But he blocked my path. My mind flashed on news stories of men breaking into houses at night. I'm used to being alone, and I instantly became afraid. I didn't know it was him. Once I reacted, it was too late. The damage was done.

"Well, he should've known. Most men know not to walk into a lady's room. What was he thinking anyhow?" Heather pats my hand.

I move on. "And all of that shit about the pond. What am I? A motel with concierge service? I didn't know how to deal with all of them at once. It's always just been just Luke and me. Sometimes we invite the girls, or our mutual friends, like you and Amber. We've always been like this. I don't know how to cater to *everyone*. There are so many. I mean, I love them, but all of them at once. I just couldn't deal with it. Does this make sense?" I hope for a little sympathy. Any sympathy will do.

"Sure, sure it does. Jeez, six of them, actually seven with Grandma Alice, and you trying to manage by yourself. It's no wonder you called me for help. It was no trouble at all, mind you, but yeah, I can see where you felt pressure to entertain, and entertain them well. I wouldn't even know where to begin. Very different, you know?"

"Yeah, it was different when we all met at their house. I just wanted to get to know them. We went out, ate dinner together, and laughed about well, all sorts of things. But here..." I take a breath. "It was a mistake. I don't know enough about them. I want to find out about them, but it's so awkward right now. Does any of this make sense?"

When I say awkward, what I really mean is scary beyond belief. I never thought much about how I was going to handle their reactions to my family and friends here. They are so new, so fresh to me. I can't begin to understand what they think. Were they focused on me or everyone gawking at them, analyzing them, and looking for traces of my gene pool in their faces?

"I think you're right. I mean they do stand out here, if you know what I mean. They're different. And they think differently than we do. After all, they're from California, and you know what they say, 'the land of fruits and nuts.' " I know Heather's trying to make me laugh, but I'm too upset.

"What do you mean by different?"

"I mean, you may look like them, but they're different from you. You were raised differently. You're like us. They're, well, so quiet. Not that there's anything wrong with being quiet, but you're not like them in personality. You've always been happy Sarah, crazy Sarah, best friend always Sarah."

"I know we're not the same. Rae is the closest to me in personality, but I still consider them my family. I hoped it would be okay for them to come to the house, but they seem like strangers here. I guess they are. All of my family and Luke's are from here. I've felt uncomfortable since they arrived. I wanted everything to be perfect, and it wasn't. Now, I just want it to be over. I feel like I don't know them at all." Tears form as frustration and exhaustion catch up with me.

She crosses her arms and nods in understanding. I'm grateful I don't always have to explain, and Heather will be here for me. I really need her right now.

"I made a mistake thinking everything would be okay. It's not okay. What he said about Mom and Dad is definitely not okay."

"What did he say?" Heather raises her eyebrows.

"He said my parents lied to me. He said they kept me away from him on purpose. What balls. My parents wouldn't do that to me. What kind of people would lie to a kid? They love me, right? I know they do." My tears threaten to spill over.

"I don't think they'd ever do that to you. Never. They've always been model parents. They even led church services when we were growing up. Remember how beautifully your mom played the guitar? Your dad was in charge of the community children's volunteer committee, remember? How could Nicholas imply they could do such a thing? Impossible."

"Yeah, that's what I thought. I called Luke. He's coming as soon as he can. I'm just so upset I can't see straight. Maybe if I talk with Sophia, things will turn around. She seems more reasonable than my—Nicholas does."

CHAPTER 43 – Sophia

This morning, Sarah took the kids to get Starbucks. I can see how excited she gets when she's around her sisters and brother. Almost like a kid at an amusement park. She waits for the next adventure to play out, marveling at the kids' words or smart aleck comments to each other. They're sweet to watch. I know she loves her brother, Rob, but our kids are new to her. It's like she's missed out on all of the fun stuff and now wants to make up for it. Missed out on *us, too.* I wonder if she feels sad when she sees us together and wonders where she was during our kids' early years. I'd probably feel more mad than sad, but I can't speak for her or know how she feels.

Nick is still angry this morning. He woke up with a migraine. They plague him when he's overworked or upset. He is so sensitive. Sometimes I wonder why he hides behind his macho facade and causes so much drama for himself and for us.

Sarah's young, and she doesn't see what we see. We barely know her world, and this is *her* world, *not ours.* Nick doesn't get it, but he'll learn the hard way. I wish he was more understanding, but he thinks with his pride, not forgiveness in his heart.

Luke's gone off to work. He spoke to Nick before he left. He's such a level-headed guy. I can't imagine what he must think of yesterday. He's probably heard it all from Sarah. She may believe Nick is upset with her. She's a spitfire. I can see where she and Rae are related. Hot tempers flare in an instant, and what starts as a small flame roars into an uncontrollable, raging inferno.

Nick has kept to himself most of the day. I'm sure Sarah senses something is wrong, but she doesn't confront him.

Her friend, Heather, drops by.

Katherine, Kaden, Nick, and I go off to the pond again. Nick and Kaden attempt to float around. Kaden doesn't approve of the slime and muddy water, but he gives it a try. I watch from the shore and take pictures of my boys.

We head back, sweaty and tired from the sun. We take turns in the shower. The cool water revives us. After lunch, we gather in the living room. Nick remains quiet and distant.

I sit against the couch and see Sarah call him out onto the porch. Windows extend the length of the porch, so I can see both of them clearly. She faces him. One hand smacks into the other, like a mother laying down the law. He listens, his shoulders tense. I can't hear what they are saying. I feel desperate, like a deaf person eyeing their lips for the shape of their words, but they speak too fast, and I get nothing. Still, it's clear to me this is not good. Tense shoulders. Motionless, except for her hands. Their body language screams through the glass.

In an instant, he darts through the glass door, slamming it as he enters. She shakes her head, like an opponent who has been defeated. I never realize until now. They have become opponents. Father and daughter.

Nick motions me to come with him. No one else seems to notice how his eyes are glazed over and tearing up.

I walk to him and place a hand on his arm.

"What's wrong? What just happened?"

"I want to go back home today. Can we please leave now? I can't stay here. I need to get out. She doesn't..." His voice breaks, whispered and fragile. "...love me."

My heart breaks for him. "Leave? Today? We're supposed to stay for a few more days. Are you sure? Let's go outside and talk. Maybe you can work this out." I want to support him, but I know our kids will be disappointed if we go.

We step out onto the paved driveway, and stand under a huge oak tree. He wears his sunglasses. The pink color around his shades warns me of the damage done.

"She doesn't love me. She told me so. I asked her straight out. She thinks I'm a creep or something. I didn't tell you this but I went to her room to talk to her last night. I pushed the door open, just like I do with our girls, and she flew into a rage. When I tried to get her to calm down she blew me off, like she was scared of me or something. I'm her dad, for Christ's sake. She just told me what she thinks of me."

By now, he was sobbing, and I was trying to piece together the story, the misunderstanding, the insult he felt as deeply as if she'd wounded him physically.

"Did you explain to her what you were doing? Maybe it doesn't happen in her family—I mean a man walking into her room. Some people are funny about these kinds of things. She doesn't know us well. Maybe she was nervous."

"I was just trying to talk to her, to explain about yesterday, and to clear the air. She talked down to me like I was a dumb child, scolding me. She said in her family they communicate by talking, even yelling, not by keeping quiet. She said they're open about how they feel. It wasn't okay for me to make her feel the way she did. I just asked her if she loves me." He takes a deep breath "She said she likes me, but she doesn't know me."

I can see there's no reasoning with him.

"Listen, let me ask your mom to talk with you for a minute. It's really going to look bad if we leave now. You know that, don't you?"

But he's tuned me out. He nods his head, but his brain speaks louder. I know his heart longs for the safety of our home in California.

I head inside and give Alice a brief summary of what's occurred. She walks out the front door. From the window, I see his mother consoling him. She appears to be crying herself as she hears his story.

The next thing I know, Alice is in the living room with the girls.

I walk to the kitchen just as Luke and Sarah enter the back door. They ask if we can talk for a minute.

Before a thought can cross my mind, Sarah starts. "What the hell just happened? I am not to blame for this.

He spooked me by walking into my room yesterday. It's not okay for him to do. When I tried to explain how things work in my family, he started bad-mouthing my parents."

I know my mouth is hanging open.

She's changed. Her quiet, sweet disposition has morphed into to this angry stranger. I listen to her rant about how it isn't acceptable for a man to walk into her room, especially a man she doesn't really know.

Then, she begins about her parents. "It is *not* okay for him to call my parents liars. They're not liars. Especially my dad. It is not okay for him to speak like that to me."

Luke tries to referee, paying particular attention to his wife. When he speaks, it's in a low, calm voice. "Sarah, watch your tone. Please try to be calm. Yelling won't help." He places a hand on her arm.

She takes a deep breath.

Dumbstruck and pinching myself to see if I'm in a nightmare, I try to explain her father's side. "Your dad told me what happened. He only wanted to talk to you. At home, he taps the door and walks in without waiting for a response. He does this with all of our kids. I know this is hard for you to understand, but he sees you as another daughter. You are part of him. He would never hurt you. You are someone he just found, and he loved you instantly. He's angry about his own lost years with you. He can't understand how different your life has been from ours. You were lost to him for twenty-six years. You are his daughter, and he feels as though he's missed most of your life." I start to cry.

She cries, too. "I like the guy, but I barely know him. He wants me to just love him completely. I already have a dad and mom. I had a great dad growing up. Nicholas expects me to forget about my whole life. I can't. He can't accept and respect my feelings."

Luke steps in, seeing how her words hurt me. They are honest, but they still hurt. I'm glad she didn't say this to Nick. "Sophia, Nicholas has done everything right. From the beginning, he connected with Sarah, got to know her, chose to love her. And you've been great about including her in your family. But, I don't see how Sarah is to blame for the situation. We love her parents, Steve and Willow. They're our family too."

"All Nick told me was he mentioned how her parents kept you away from him. I find it hard to believe he'd call them liars. From the beginning, he's only wanted to protect you from any more pain. If he said these things, it was only because he's upset. He'd never intentionally say anything to hurt you."

Luke wraps an arm around Sarah. "I suggest we take a break. Sarah, come out to the farm with me. Sophia, maybe you can talk to Nicholas a little more and see if he comes around. Then we can meet later and discuss this situation when we're all calmer."

"Yes, it might help everyone cool off."

The two head out and down the path toward the barn.

I join Nick where he remains under the tree. "I just spoke with Sarah and Luke. Babe, did you call her parents liars? She said you did." I study Nick's face.

"I said her parents kept her away from me all these years. I was angry, but I never called them liars." His fingers press his temple.

"Well, I guess she interpreted your statement as something else. She and Luke went out to the farm. Do you still want to leave? They want us to talk about this later, after everyone has calmed down."

I leave out the rest of the conversation since talking to the wall in front of me is useless.

"I need to get out of here. I feel like I'm going to go crazy." The skin around his eyes, around his sunglasses, looks red and swollen.

*****

Alice tries once more to get him to come around.

She comes back, and I can tell he's still adamant.

She shakes her head. "He says he wants to go, even though I told him I think he's making a big mistake. He might never be welcomed back. But he says he has to leave, so what should we do?"

"I don't want to tell the kids too much, just that their father and sister had a misunderstanding and we're leaving early. I guess we'll clear up our stuff and go."

I call Carissa and Katherine and tell them to pack. They look puzzled, but don't ask questions. They can see from our expressions something serious is happening. Everyone cleans the upstairs rooms. Alice and I pull wet laundry out of the washer and dump the clothes into clean garbage bags.

My family is uncharacteristically quiet as we gather our clothes, remake the beds, wash and put away every dish.

The kids take our bags to the van while Alice and I check the rooms. I nearly cry when I see the special places Sarah decorated for her new siblings. *She went to such trouble. Oh, God, how did it go so wrong?*

We leave the house exactly how we found it. We want to leave Sarah no further reason to resent us.

We take care of everything within an hour. With the car packed and ready to go, I count heads and notice one missing.

"Where's Kat?"

"I think she took a walk in the orchard," Carissa says. "She knows we're leaving."

I walk toward the backyard with its plush green grass and immaculate flower beds. I enter the orchard of intricate perfectly manicured trees. There, in the Y of an apricot tree, sits Kat. She's crying.

"Kat, it's time to go, baby."

"I don't want to go. Why did Dad have to pick a fight with her?" She sobs.

"It's complicated. They had a misunderstanding, and they have to work it out, but Dad is very upset. We have to leave now."

"We'll never see her again. I don't want to leave."

"It might be a while before we see them again, but for right now, Daddy can't stay here. He feels a great deal of pain over what happened."

And as my baby girl cries, I hold her. A soft breeze moves through the orchard. Speckled light from the sun peers through the leaves.

What Kat says is true. I don't want to lie to her, but I know staying here isn't going to make things better for Nick. I don't want Sarah and Luke to watch us go.

We hug each other and then slowly walk back to the car. As we drive away, my heart breaks for my husband, for myself, and our kids, for Sarah and Luke. Nick leaves a message on Luke's phone, thanking him.

Nick ends his message, "I'm sorry things ended like this. You are a great man, Luke."

What will become of our family now?

We leave at two in the afternoon and stop to eat a late lunch/early dinner. Nick sits and cries quietly as the kids go to the bathroom. After ordering our food, he takes the two older girls outside. I have no idea what he intends to say to them.

On the road again, I receive a text from Sarah saying Rae sent a nasty text to her telling her about how great her dad is and how much he loves them. She told Sarah she hadn't spent much time with a man who loved her so much, even though he'd gone a long way to see her. He had not rejected her, so why was she was treating him this way?

I return her text. "Let's take a break for a while and let things settle down. Anger makes all of us say things we don't mean."

By the next rest stop, Luke has left a message on Nick's phone. He hands me the phone.

I look at his broken face, take the phone, and listen to the message:

"My wife is on the bed, ready to die. I don't understand how you could leave without saying goodbye. We wanted to work things out, but you just left. I don't understand. It didn't have to be like this. And what about the kids? We didn't want to involve them. I just don't get it. Please call when you can. This is very disappointing."

"What should I do?" Nick looks at me like a small boy who threw a baseball through a window and watched the glass shatter.

What should we do? What should we do? You've done enough already.

"Don't call him back. You're still too upset, and we don't need anything else to be misinterpreted. And the girls, babe? Really? They didn't need to know everything."

"They needed to know what she thought of me." He sounded like a child in a "he said she said" fight.

"No, they didn't. They are just kids. If you ever decide to reconcile with her and Luke, the kids may still hold grudges. They don't know what to do with these emotions."

He's quiet, for once, and I take his silence to mean he won't call Luke back. I breathe in the last of the Washington air and get into the van. It will be a long ride home.

There isn't a dry eye in the car as we drive straight through the night. Only fitful sleep stops the tears. It's as if someone has died. We weep for ourselves, for the uncertainty we feel about the future. Our minds and hearts ache. Sarah had been lost to him for so long, and now, she's gone again. We've come so far with her and now, it's over. It's a kind of death—the death of our relationship, the death of our family.

When I wake in the afternoon, I attack the chores. I'm still in my pajamas as I survey the mess and move around the quiet house. I entered Kaden's room only to find it empty since he slept on the couch.

Nick comes to me. "I feel *so* bad." He looks down at the ground, his expression filled with sorrow, apology, defeat.

"I know, babe. I know."

"So what do you think about what happened?" He seems rested and in touch with reality.

I sigh. "I think we made a huge mistake by leaving, but we'll have to see how things go. I can't imagine what they think of us."

To me, what we did was equivalent of leaving someone at the altar and watching them cry as you drove away. We hurt people we care about, and it feels so wrong. But, as I look at my husband with his sad face, I know he doesn't need any more criticism or logic from me. I hug him and hope time, the great healer, will eventually improve things.

*****

Throughout July and then August, my tearful face greets me in the mirror each morning. My tears fall on waking up and resume when I retire for the night.

I rarely cry, so I don't know how or why I can't stop now. I just know life has changed after our time with Sarah, and I miss her. It feels like a kind of death. I grieve for her.

I witnessed a miracle. Someone disclosed the truth, and we felt something wonderful. Now it is gone, like the stars when they disappear behind a cloud. Sarah's still out there, but we can't see her.

I only cry alone in the quiet of my room. As the moon and stars light the world, my tears join my prayers to reconcile with Sarah and Luke. I pray for Nick and Sarah in an almost rosary-like way, bead after bead, night after night, wishing for God's miracle to take away my tears and bring back the hope I'd witnessed in their union, father and daughter.

PART IV– STARTING OVER AGAIN

CHAPTER 44 – Nicholas

School has begun, and like any new year, it brings change. What hasn't changed is the ache in my heart. The one only Sophia understands.

Since my blowup with Sarah and our return to Eastville, I've worked on our new yard, replacing sprinkler heads, pulling out dead plants and weeds, and tearing down and building up new structures. I work from six in the morning until dinner, and then I go to my bedroom and crash. It's how I survive, survive another day without her.

My tears mix with the dirt on my face, but no one sees. I'm sure Sophia knows, but she never says anything. She feels my pain. I'm torn, almost desperate over Sarah.

At times, I secretly wish my life could go back to the way it was before Sarah came into it. I know this isn't possible. I can't just erase her. Other men may be able to forget, but I can't. Maybe others believe my facade. I try to appear as solid as a brick wall, impervious to the hurt I feel.

We continue to attend Mass at Our Lady of Miracles, and every service echoes the same word—*forgive*. I continue to receive communion. Even though I've gone to confession, I'm not ready to let go of the hurt which tears at my being. Deep down, I try to do what God wants of me, but my emotions take over the logic of my mind. It's like a million people beat me down, except the only person who's done this is my daughter, my first born. I try to get over it by myself. I pray, but at the mention of her name I scowl. My family has stopped talking about her.

I'm determined not to let her hurt me again. I'm worn down from bitterness. I can't think about her, my daughter.

Sophia has been quiet for months. Gradually, she's started to mention Sarah. She lost someone close to her, but it feels like *she* wants Sarah back more than I do. I don't understand.

I want to beat the crap out of someone when I think of all of this anger inside me.

Sophia reminds me to think about what Father John says to us: "Forgive, forgive, forgive." Every week, the same message. My mind understands, but my heart doesn't want to listen. They have become strangers.

CHAPTER 45 – Sophia

I've been in a trance for months. Tears flow every morning for no reason. I feel sad for all of us

I finally reach out to Sarah. It's now early fall. Enough time has gone by for her to have cooled down. The defensiveness she felt this summer was so intense, so sudden. I don't see how she could have taken offense at what I said. I hope she'll listen to me, even if she wouldn't to her father.

I email her one afternoon and let it all out: the way she was with her father, the way we responded to her, the loss we felt upon returning home. I need to get it out. I feel like I've lost a child.

I don't hear back from her. This may be a bad sign.

Nick has been stoic. He's hiding his emotions, but I know they run deep and strong. He loves his daughter, even if he pretends he doesn't care. He doesn't fool me. Every day since we returned from Washington, he's worked himself ragged. He comes in, showers, eats, and falls asleep.

He's hurting all right, but he wants us to think he doesn't care anymore.

Only, I'm not stupid. I know my husband. Somewhere beyond his sullen, stoic and brave demeanor, he's devastated at the way they left each other. He has so much compassion and concern for others, so it doesn't fit. It's not like him to leave without resolving the issue.

He made the decision in the heat of the moment because anger won out over love.

From years of loving him, despite his faults, I know his deepest feelings. He loves me despite my failings and insecurities, too. I can see what he can't.

Although perhaps he isn't ready to admit it, his disappointment is mostly in himself.

CHAPTER 46 – Katherine

I have a secret. My secret is Sarah. I miss her. I miss her so much, and I don't understand why everyone can't just make things go back to the way they were before. I text her once in a while, and she always answers back.

We never bring up Dad, because that would just be too awka-awkward. I'm so glad she answers because I don't want her to think we don't love her anymore. I mean, we're family. We're supposed to love each other through everything. Rae and Carissa fight with me sometimes, and we always get over it. We pretend to be annoyed with each other for weeks, and then one good day comes, and we're sisters again, like nothing ever happened. It's the way family should be—close. I wish Sarah lived closer to us so I could hug her. I think she needs us.

On my birthday, she told me a surprise was coming for me. At school, they delivered a small bouquet of flowers to my room. Everyone ran to see who sent it to me. I was so happy to get something from Sarah. I know her birthday is right around the corner.

When I bring the flowers home, I set them on the kitchen island.

Right away, my dad asks, "Who are those from?"

"Sarah."

He just harrumphs and walks out of the room. Again, awka-awkward.

I ask Mom if I can send Sarah a present. You know, for her birthday in October. I don't know if anyone else will remember, but I want her to get a gift from me. I want her to know we haven't forgotten about her.

Mom is sorta nervous, not because she's holding grudges, but because she wants us to keep it between us. She doesn't know if Dad will approve.

I decide to tell Mom my secret. "I've been texting Sarah for a while now. Is it wrong of me, Mom?"

"No, it's not wrong at all. You can text her as much as you want." Mom nods and smiles. "I'm proud of you for choosing to love and understand Sarah."

I don't like keeping secrets. Now that Mom knows, I feel great.

CHAPTER 47 – Alice

I have prayed for them, Nicky, Sophia, Sarah. It has been months since we left Sarah and Luke's farm. I can still remember pulling all the wet laundry out of the machine, packing the clothes in new garbage bags, and rushing to get out of their house.

When I went outside to talk to Nicky, I could tell he was deeply hurt. He has always been emotional, much like my father. Sarah saying she didn't love him was too much for him.

My Nicky, he has a big heart.

I still remember the day he asked me and Brianna to meet him at my house. We sat at my kitchen table, and he started crying. Brianna and I cried with him. I panicked. The worst scenarios came to me. *My boy is sick. Cancer? His heart? What else could it be?*

As he explained about Willow and Sarah, I could tell he was overwhelmed by his emotions. *Another daughter.*

Brianna and I were stunned.

As for Willow, I can't recall her. Many girls had crushes on my boy. Everyone loved my Nicky. He was so handsome, but he was also compassionate and listened with his heart. He's had this quality since childhood. Now, as a man, he hasn't lost this gift. When he learned about a child he had created and had no part in raising, I feared his sorrow and resentment would stay with him for a long time.

Sophia is very strong. I knew she was strong enough to go out on her own if she chose to. She'd never leave the kids, but she could manage alone with her kids if she needed to. Taking on an adult stepdaughter was a huge undertaking—accepting a child from another woman. She wasn't one to cause a scene, but I could understand how upset she must be. Only a truly good person could move beyond such a startling revelation. Sophia is a good person.

When Nicky told us Sophia had accepted Sarah, I thought, *Thank goodness for God's love.* Everything came down to God's love telling them to do the right thing. Sophia has been alongside Nicky through everything else, so I wasn't surprised when she supported him in this situation.

Of all of my children, Nicky and Sophia, are the only ones married in the Catholic Church. They are adamant their children will follow in their faith. Although I know a church wedding doesn't guarantee a lasting marriage, their faith has sustained them. I can see a difference in their lives and in their children.

The day of the disaster at Sarah and Luke's, I knew Nicky was making a big mistake. In the beginning, he wanted to know her and learn about her life. In a short time, we were driving to Washington.

We were strangers to Sarah and Luke. It must have been hard for her to welcome us into her home.

Then we left suddenly over a misunderstanding. In my eyes, it could have been worked out with love and patience. Unfortunately Nicky's anger outweighed his patience. I know my son. Once he's hurt, he stays hurt for a while. There is no reasoning with him.

I went out to try to talk sense into him. He was upset, and his emotions poured out. "She doesn't love me. She doesn't want me as her parent."

I listened and tried to understand, and I cried along with him. What else was I to do? Listen and understand. That's what mothers do.

So when I couldn't get him to budge, he didn't care to hear what I had to say. I warned him, "You might not be welcomed back, son." He folded his arms and looked away.

I went inside and helped Sophia and the girls clean up and pack. We knew he was hurting and wanted to get away. Even though Sophia and I knew better, we weren't going to argue with him.

On the drive home, I heard the sniffles, and I knew everyone had been affected. No one talked on that long ride home. Just hours and hours of sleeping and weeping. It's what I remember most about our drive home. Silence and pain filled the van. Sarah had broken Nicky's heart.

I've finally worked up the nerve to call her. A few months have passed, and I hope she may be ready to forgive us.

She seems tentative, quiet. She says she considers me her grandma and did as soon as I met her, so I hope I have some influence. In reality, I don't know her very well, and I'm not sure it's my place to interfere. However, I'm still her grandma, and Nicky is still my son, so I say what I need to say.

I hope I sound confident. "How are you doing? It's been a couple of months since we've heard from you."

"I know, Grandma. I just needed some time to sort through all of this."

"It probably was too soon for both of you. Nicky loved you in an instant. He has a big heart and loves his family. You are part of his family, you know."

"Yes, I know." She speaks so softly I barely understand her words. "I hate the way things ended. I was just so mixed up with all of these new emotions. I really wanted all of you, *new Dad*, Sophia, the kids, to be with Luke and me, but then when you got here, it was just—well, too much. I didn't know what to do or say. It was confusing for me."

"I imagine so. It was too soon for both of you. My son, your dad, he loves you just like his other children. You hurt him terribly. I hope sometime soon, you'll reconnect with him. It's not good to leave this unsettled. You are family."

"I shouldn't have said what I said. I wasn't ready to take such a big step—loving him. I know I hurt him."

"Yes, you did. He was deeply hurt, but time will help him. Just make sure you connect with him again. When you're ready."

"He's great, and I know he loves me. It's hard to understand everything. I need more time for all of this to sink in. I discovered too late that it was too soon for me. I know we should connect again."

I end with, "I love you."

She promises to call me soon.

It will take Nicky a long time to heal. I know my boy.

CHAPTER 48 - Sophia

Kids simply amaze me. As much as I work with them as a teacher, I'm most amazed at my own.

Katherine is wise beyond her years. Once as a two year old, she witnessed a small girl throwing a tantrum in Target. I didn't say a word, but she gave me a confused look.

"Why is she acting that way, Mommy?"

"I don't know, but it looks like she's not listening to her mommy."

"No, she isn't."

"What do you think would happen if you acted like that with me?"

"I guess, you'd spank me, Mommy." She sounded matter-of-fact. "But I'm a good girl and I behave. You've never spanked me."

"That's right, but I know you wouldn't act like that, right? You know what we expect of you?"

"Yes, Mommy. I wouldn't be like that girl."

She never misbehaved as a child. She was my bright light, always loving and smiling, much like my other children. After every meal I prepared for her, she thanked me.

So her reconnection with Sarah doesn't surprise me.

Katherine has taken the initiative to follow her heart. She wasn't too proud to make the first move, unlike the grownups around her.

I'm curious. *What does she say to Sarah now since things ended so abruptly? How do they get along?*

I try not to ask too many questions because I don't want Katherine to clam up. Instead, she asks about Sarah's birthday. Will I take her to buy a gift for her sister? Will Dad get mad when he finds out?

I tell her, "Yes, of course we'll go and pick out something for her. We'll send it before her birthday so she gets it on time."

*****

Sarah's birthday passes like any other day. Nick and I teach our classes. At home, we eat dinner, clean up the house, and take our showers. Nick lies in bed and watches TV. He appears emotionless, focused on a game of some sort. He doesn't let on, but I know Sarah's on his mind. I know my husband.

I'm hesitant to bring up her name, so I decide to leave it alone. Only I can't. I can't just leave something alone that should be so good. So good for him, for her, and for our family. It tears at me...

It's nine-thirty. I head to the kitchen to eat a bowl of Cap'n Crunch cereal. *Munch, munch.* I sit at the granite island in the middle of the kitchen in the dark. *Munch, munch.* My toes curl around the cold metal of the bar stool. I look at my cell phone and the lit screen. *Take a chance, Sophia. Hmm... What do I say?*

CHAPTER 49 – Nicholas

Damn it. My day was going perfectly fine until that simple little text. I'm ending the day watching the game in bed and then the whistle sounds from my cell. I pick up the phone and read the text. Damn it. Why can't she just leave it alone?

"You know, babe, today is your dad's birthday. It's also your daughter's birthday. It's not too late to wish her happy birthday. Don't waste time. Start over again. ~Sophia~"

I was just about to settle in for the night, even though I knew I wasn't going to sleep. It's true. Dad's birthday is today. He passed in 1992 when Sarah would have been around eleven. Today is her birthday, twenty-seven years too late. She's been on my mind all day, like a recurring tune I couldn't get out of my head. How many birthdays has she celebrated without me?

Brick by brick, the wall I've built starts to crumble.

Sophia is like my conscience, like Jiminy Cricket in the cartoon. She rests on my shoulder and speaks her mind, not making demands, but confident, sensible, matter-of-fact. The voice I don't want to hear when I *really* want to be stubborn and insist I'm right. I know I can't ignore her, because I know what she says is true. Her words get to me.

I find Sarah's contact number and text in my message:

"It's your birthday today. Happy Birthday, Sarah. I haven't forgotten about you."

In less than half a minute, she replies:

"Thank you, Dad. This was my BEST present by far today."

When Sophia comes into our bedroom, she walks past me like she has done nothing.

I stop her with my hand on her arm. I look her in the eye, pull off my reading glasses, and say, "All because of you." I show her the text I sent and Sarah's reply.

Sophia smiles, hugs me, and climbs into bed.

As we turn out the lights, I know the woman beside me is smiling in the dark. Although I'd like to hate her for making me reach out to Sarah, I can't do it. Her love overwhelms me as I turn, put my arm around her, and kiss her goodnight.

CHAPTER 50 – Brianna

She's been texting me since the trip to Washington. My look-alike niece needed to talk. When I first met her, I did a double-take to make sure I wasn't looking in a mirror. Sophia and Nick had told me she looked like me, but oh my goodness. They were so right. Now, I have this connection with her we can't describe. She's an Aldana for sure.

Sarah began texting me a month or so after her fight with Nick. Again and again, I heard her say (without words), "*He* did this and *he* said that." Never did she say, "*I* shouldn't have done..." or "*I* shouldn't have said..."

After a few exchanges, I finally just come out with it. I write:

"You know I love you, and I wouldn't say anything to hurt you because you're family now. I know I don't know you very well, but I must say this. It was too soon, for both of you. I think it was overwhelming for you, and my brother expected emotions you weren't prepared to express yet. It's easy to see from the outside, but for him, it wasn't. He sees you as his daughter, but you still see a stranger who is your biological father. He was wrong for the way he left things, but you were wrong, too. He is your father. He's blood, and nothing will ever change that. You can't deny this fact. I know it's hard to accept, especially since you believed your whole life Steve was your real dad. My brother is your father, and he loves you even though he's being a hardhead right now. I can tell you are just as stubborn as he is. You are an Aldana."

I wait for a response, and shortly, she replies:

"Thanks, *Tia* Brianna."

*****

Back and forth over the next few months, we text. Eventually, reading between the lines, I sense a change of heart. Her words are not so negative. She seeks guidance, understanding.

I'm an outsider in this situation, yet I'm still family. She's stubborn all right, and coming to me must have been awkward for her. Then again, I'm not Sophia, and I'm not my brother, so maybe that's why it's okay for her to listen to me.

CHAPTER 51 – Sarah

I'm so relieved. *New Dad* texted me. I mean my *dad* texted me on my birthday. I'm still getting used to using the term "dad" for him, because I still think of Steve as Dad. But *Tia* Brianna is right. I have to accept that I am an Aldana, and it's okay to get close to Nicholas.

I just wasn't ready. I thought I was, but I was in way over my head. The emotions, the expectations, the comments... I felt like my head was spinning when Dad and the family arrived. It hit me—these people are now my family. Although part of me was excited, another part just felt wrong.

What about my other life? My parents? My friends? My life? What do I do with this other life? Who will I become when I'm with them or without them? All these questions swarmed in my mind like millions of bees around a hive.

When my Aldana family arrived, it was as if someone took a bat to the hive, and swung. Bees flew about, dazed, confused, terrified, wondering where to go. The home they'd always known was gone. In my head, the bees buzzed in the background, disturbing my peace, and making me feel lost in chaos.

Now, Dad's made the first move. I feel relieved. I know he was furious at me, and I was scared of rejection if I contacted him. I recognized the same fear as when I finally decided to try to find him. Deep down, I feared he'd deny me, turn me away, never want me to be part of his life.

Now, I remember our first emails and talks. He was so loving, so genuine. I was overwhelmed to think he could love me without ever knowing me.

I so wanted to fit in with everyone, and for a time, it was great.

Well, now we are starting again. I still feel angry at the way things ended, but I'm also embarrassed. I could have done or said things differently, but I was so mixed up. No one could have understood unless they were in my position. Even Luke, as supportive and understanding as he was, couldn't understand how mixed up I was.

New beginnings are so hard, so humbling. I want to believe things will go back to where they were when we were happy and loved each other.

CHAPTER 52 – Sophia

Christmas has come and gone. The kids were happy with their presents. We sent Sarah and Luke their gifts in the mail: a scarf, warm beanie, and gift cards for her, and pajamas, warm gloves, and a hat for him. Everyone contributed to their package, and we felt pleased with our choices, but we'd really liked to have seen them up close.

It's now close to Easter, and Sarah says she wants to visit.

Nick's communicated more with her in these past months, and it seems a change has occurred. They've developed a closeness they didn't have before.

Carissa requests to leave when Sarah comes. She's our stubborn one, just like dear old Dad. The last to accept, the last to trust. The latter trait comes more from me than from her father.

As I read the mound of senior class essays on my lap, the conversation begins.

"Has Dad talked to her? To Sarah?"

"Yes, your dad has been texting her, talking to her since her birthday." I turn to face her.

"Since her birthday? I thought he was mad at her. I thought we all were, at least when we left. How come no one said anything to me?" She raises her voice. "Don't we get a say as to whether or not she comes back into our lives?"

"Maybe we didn't say anything, Carissa, because we knew you'd made up your mind. It was done. You were through with her, but she's still family, whether you like it or not. In this family you don't get to choose. Maybe in other families it's different, but not in ours."

I could tell my words weren't registering in the idealistic, logical brain of my straight-A student. She didn't respond.

"We were all upset when we left, but I think things just happened way too fast. Your dad expected more than Sarah was ready to give, and it hurt him. He's stubborn, too. He doesn't forgive easily."

"Well, can I go visit Grandma or someone while she's here? I don't want to be here." She sounded resolute.

"During Easter break? Carissa, you need to forgive her. Dad is trying not to let this one situation overshadow something good. We need to make the effort for him. I know you're a hardhead, just like him. We need to give her another chance."

"So that's it? That's how it is? We don't get a say at all?" She storms out.

As she climbs the stairs to her room, I hear the thud of each step. She doesn't shout, "I'm pissed off," or swear like some teenagers might have.

She goes into her purple, OCD designed room, with Shirtless Man peering down, and closes the door.

With a sigh of frustration, I take a deep breath and go back to reading the essay I'd been grading.

CHAPTER 53 – Nicholas

She's coming. Sarah is on her way. I don't know how to feel. Part of me is still stubborn and defensive. *I'm going to tell her what I think about her parents. I'm still letting her know it wasn't okay for them to keep us apart. It'll never be okay as far as I'm concerned.*

The rest of me is all mush, loving, wanting to hug her again, just like the first time. Although I feel this way, I know one thing for certain—I'll never return to Washington, no matter what. Her life is there. It will remain there. She can visit us. It won't disrupt her life so much. Yes, this is for the best.

The entire family, including Carissa, who hasn't said a word about Sarah, packs up the car, and we head to the Santa Ava Airport. We look at the big screen TV which shows the faces of people as they come off of the plane. For about ten minutes, we squint at the fuzzy screen and point to possibilities.

"No, that's not her. She's way too big. She fills up the screen," Kaden says.

"Maybe the one with the pants and blue shirt?" Carissa points.

"No, she's way too tall. Think midget size." Rae laughs.

Katherine grins. "There she is, with the sweater. It looks like her face."

Finally. She's one of the last people to exit. We see her purple rolling luggage and a purse. Yes, she's wearing a sweater and a scarf.

I'm the first to hug her. She drops all of her things as she sees my face. We whisper our apologies to each other. Then everyone else takes a turn at hugging her. Even Carissa hugs her tight.

"Oh my gosh, how you've grown. Both of you." She looks at Katherine, who now towers over her big sister, and Kaden, who wraps his arm around her waist.

"So much to catch up on. I'm glad to see all of you." Sarah beams.

We load up the van, and head back for the forty-five minute drive to Eastville. As I look in the rearview mirror, my picture is complete—all four girls and my boy talking, laughing, cutting each other down a notch or two. I smile. *Yes, it's a sweet ride home.*

CHAPTER 54 – Sarah

I wanted to cry (*I did cry*) on the first glimpse of my family. They stand there, waiting for me, Aldana style. *How could I ever have let them leave?* Closing my eyes, I think back to the day of the argument, and returning to my empty house.

The quiet was the first indication of something wrong.

No giggles, no laughter, just lonely silence. The same silence filled many of my days when Luke was out on the farm, only this was much worse. I remember running from room to room, frantically looking for them, running down the basement stairs, hoping Grandma was in the spare room.

I waited for them to return. Every room was spotless. No sign of them remained, except for a pair of Katherine's shorts down the side of the bed.

They'd left me. As panic set in, I ran upstairs, crying hysterically, throwing myself at Luke. He led me into our bedroom, and comforted me as best he could. I cried in big, bellowing heaves until I thought I might die of a broken heart. I felt as though like I'd lost a loved one, only I'd lost my entire family.

The only comparable feeling I could remember was way back when my parents had a terrible fight. I remember my mom walking away and leaving me, leaving us. Since I was a child, I didn't understand everything going on between my parents. I knew my mom was upset, and I hoped she'd come home, but I wasn't sure. Luckily, she returned a few hours later after cooling off. This same sense of abandonment returned as I searched the house for Nicholas, Sophia, and my siblings. Their abandonment was like a death to me.

This is the scenario I had feared when I first contacted him. *He doesn't want me. They don't want me to be a part of their family. I don't belong.*

Where did they go? Why is everything returned to its normal place? The house is clean, spotless, and sterile. It was just a misunderstanding, a fight. My Washington family argues all the time. It's normal to me. We air our differences and come away clean and ready to start again.

I sighed and began to sob once more at having lost him, lost all of them. *What have I done?*

Luke tried to call Dad, but all he could do was leave a message. He tried reason, describing how heartbroken I was, how he didn't understand what had taken place. He asked why we couldn't just talk it out.

I lay in bed, curled into fetal position, hoping I would disappear because I felt like nothing. *My own family doesn't want me. They couldn't make the effort to work things out. I'm not worth it.*

Now, as I look at my family, the one we (Dad and I) had split apart for so many months, I wonder why I thought I'd lost them.

Sighing with relief, I melt into their arms and back into their lives. I vow things will change for the better. I can't lose them again.

CHAPTER 55 – Sophia

They text every day now. My husband and his daughter are finally bonding.

After Sarah's Easter visit, our relationship has been different. We have been different. I'm not jealous. I see their relationship as new and refreshed, changed.

Periodically, I ask, "How's Sarah?"

He responds, "She's fine. Haven't heard much from her lately."

Maybe he wants her to himself. They seem closer now. I'm glad she is with us again.

It's a new year, and the days fly by faster than I can count.

Life in our household hasn't changed much except that her senior year is very busy for Rae and me. Applications, college paperwork, what a mess. Besides the regular everyday piles of senior essays I grade, I'm sorting through college forms and applications to meet her due dates. So many forms with specific details and necessary requirements.

Rae shut down days ago as far as filling in these papers, so here I am with the mess in front of me. Mental breakdown isn't far off.

It's the beginning of April, and I call Sarah. "Pray for me, okay? I have so much to do and so little energy these days. Keep praying for me until the end of the school year. I need to feel Him helping me."

"I'll pray every day, okay? Love you, Sophia."

I disconnect and smile, grateful to have her in my life again.

When I look at my appointment calendar, every day, every hour has something planned, scheduled, or to be scheduled. I breathe in a deep sigh and say, "Help me Lord. I'll need You these next few months."

And as the days pass and the dates are crossed off, I feel like He's carried me through this crazy, impossible time. I know Sarah's prayers have helped. I couldn't do these tasks by myself.

*****

Graduation Day is here. My daughter is going into the big world, and I'm so happy for her yet sad inside to know she'll be making decisions on her own without me. I knew today would come, but never thought it would arrive so quickly. I can't say I haven't been stressed out, but the day is finally here, and I'm so relieved.

Rae sings the National Anthem with her quartet of friends, Nancy, Rianna, and Shanda. I realize it's her last performance at Eastville High School. All of the choir concerts and performances with Ms. Miller as her instructor are over. I will truly miss these moments.

As I sit in the dusk watching the stage brighten with the stadium lights, I savor this moment with her, her teachers, and her family. I watch her accept her diploma which proclaims to the world she has made it. I'm so proud. Once she leaves the stage, she walks toward me seated near the other Eastville teachers. I'm the first to receive a hug after this great moment.

I wonder how Sarah feels about being included in this experience. She is here for her sister's graduation, but we've missed out on all of her triumphs. I'm sure she's glad to be here, but deep down, I wonder if she's sad because her siblings missed her greatest accomplishments—high school graduation, college graduation, marriage. Time has no rewind button. If we could return in time to be present for her, we would. But reality is reality. She will never know what she missed at these times. Neither will we.

I decide I'm grateful she is here and part of our family milestone.

After the ceremony, Sarah hugs and kisses all of us. She is joyous, beaming.

Rae jumps into the arms of Johnny, my nephew from Arizona, along with my other nephew, Chris. They are crazy excited about the entire evening and so glad she is finished with school. Rae climbs onto Johnny's shoulders, and the two go hollering, running around the field, typical teenagers.

My sister, Monica, and my brother-in-law, Phillip, congratulate her. The senior photographer at the Arizona Running Newspaper, Phillip offers his skills to record this moment since, in the rush of the evening, my camera remains on the floor in my bedroom, unused and untouched. We pose as a family—Sarah, Rae, Carissa, Katherine, Kaden, Nick, and I. It is our first picture together since the argument. Our first family portrait.

*****

This morning, the girls set up the tables, which have been delivered on the side of the house. In the heat of the day, they wipe them down, unfold the chairs, lay out the tablecloths, and arrange the chair covers.

By this evening, the backyard is transformed into a fairyland of black and red, her school colors, with red tablecloths and black runners down the center of the tables. We've added some blue in other decorations for Johnny's school colors, since he, too, graduated and his family joins us tonight from Los Pastores. The chairs are covered in black and tied with beautiful satin ribbons. As centerpieces, we place picture frames, each with specially chosen pictures from the past, Rae and Johnny as infants, all of the Aldana crew, the Cuevas boys, Rae and her friends, Johnny and his girlfriend, Priscilla, and Sarah and the kids. Next to the centerpieces are flameless candles. So economical yet so classy, they sparkle, turning our plain back yard into an elegant bistro. Above the white lattice near the pool, white twinkle lights glitter in the darkness, and the trickling water from the pool's waterfall makes the night seem like a dream.

Our guests arrive. Even as busy as I am, I wonder how Sarah feels about everything. *Does she feel included? Is she feeling left out with all of the commotion?* She's helped all day long in the hot sun and now is as beautiful as ever as she laughs with the rest of our kids. As I get the food ready to take out, I'm not sure she's met everyone or if she's just being polite as people walk in.

I eventually make my way to a table where Nick and his cousins, The Velazquez girls, sit with Sarah. Alice is next to her. Like a proud grandma, she tells everyone Sarah's story. They glance at me, smile, and continue listening.

The cousins say they can't believe such a miracle came about. They're delighted. She is an Aldana all right.

Cousin Fernando Aldana at first thinks Sarah is another cousin he never met since she looks like the Aldana family, but he just can't remember her name. When the story reaches him, he stares from Nick to Sarah.

"I need another beer," he announces.

Others meet Sarah for the first time. My parents and brother, Marcos and his girlfriend, arrive to greet her. Cousins from my side of the family, who've heard the story are struck by her resemblance to their children.

They gather around along with other *tia*s and *tio*s from my side.

Many of our friends attend to share this special occasion with us.

After the cakes are cut, marble cake for Rae and *tres leches* for Johnny, family and friends mingle and savor the night air. It's been very hot throughout the day, so the cool evening is welcome.

Nick's friends from high school sit near the pool reminiscing with Nick about Jimmy's Pizzeria and Los Pastores High School.

I sit with Phillip and Monica. They ask me what life is like with Sarah as part of the family.

I explain the story again, and it feels normal. I think they can tell I accept her as another daughter in my life. She is part of our family.

As I reflect on the celebration and the family embracing not only Rae's graduation, but our other daughter, Sarah, it makes me grateful for the love others have shown. I'm thankful for the strength which has seen us through and brought us to this moment.

Sarah looks happy and content with *Tia* Brianna and *Tio* Benito, Kiera, Seth, little Kendra, Grandma Alice, and the Aldana cousins. For a young woman who started out so alone in the beginning, so scared of disrupting our quiet world, she is now surrounded by loving family members who accept and love her without reservation.

CHAPTER 56– Nicholas

I look across the yard and there she is, my Sarah. How I wish things could have been different, but time has been a friend to me. Time has made me stronger. I couldn't see past the hate and anger, and I didn't want to forgive. But, when I see my daughter, my firstborn, I can honestly say time must have brought her to me at the right time. Not in my time, of course, but in God's time. He must have known what I couldn't fathom.

Although my heart will always long for what I missed in her life, I can see God's plan now. The way things fell together for Sophia, the kids, my extended family. Everyone can love Sarah with no exceptions. I am learning to let go of my anger and sense of betrayal. I'm not sure if all of the anger will ever disappear, but the closure I need is here tonight, in this moment.

Surrounded by family and friends, I am awestruck by the love a family can give to one another, especially to me. I know some may not believe I was the young naïve boy who brought Sarah into the world, but they love me and her with forgiveness and acceptance. It feels right to move onto a new life with her.

CHAPTER 57 – Sarah

As I watch Rae graduate on the Eastville High football field, I know exactly what I've missed with my new family. My heart sinks for all the events I'll never know.

Sophia is dressed in her teacher robe, sitting near the aisle with the soon-to-be Eastville High graduates.

I see Rae run to her mom after she receives her diploma. They embrace in front of her peers.

After the ceremony, my new family runs to greet my sister, with hugs and kisses, pictures, and smiles. I recognize *Tio* Phillip and *Tia* Monica, and my new cousins, Johnny and Chris. Under the lights of the stadium, all of their radiant faces look happy and excited. Seeing this huge family surround their newest graduate with joy and love makes tears come to my eyes.

They were missing from all my life milestones. I think about graduations, parties, celebrations. None of these people were with me. I replay these times in my head and think how wonderful it would have been for them to be a part of these special times with me. They could not share my joys or my sorrows. How I would have loved to join them around the table for a good meal and conversation with my little brother and sisters.

Then I feel betrayed, sorrowful, and yet grateful. I'm part of them now. We are making new memories together.

They loved me without knowing me. *How could they?* Without knowing anything about me, they welcomed me in their home. They fed me, entertained me, and surprised me with grand gestures. Their hugs came with no hesitation or awkwardness, their words spoke kindness and understanding, and their actions showed there were no differences between us. The warmth my sisters gave me in my dark moments saw me through.

Likewise, I've laughed with them in happy times, the few memories we now share.

I now know the gift of their love. I came to it late—twenty-six years late. I wish I could go back in time. My life would have been blessed more so if they had shared it.

I wonder if I would have been different. I try to imagine. Maybe I'd have been more like them, more centered, more faithful, and calm. The first part of my life, with its turmoil and the chaos of my parents' divorce, was a lesson—a lesson on how to love myself and my family, flawed as we are. We're just like any other family, imperfect yet accepting of one another.

I've had to deal with choices made by those who loved me most. Choices I now wish had been made differently. Despite their mistakes, I know my parents love me, and I love them.

However, what they did to change my life ultimately created pain. Now, before my eyes, I see all of the love I missed in my early years.

It is vivid and real, and displayed before me. Inside, my soul cries silent tears for what I've lost. I long to see what might have been, had I known of them sooner.

I finally understand what Dad meant when he said he lost me, because now I realize he was lost to me, too.

When Dad and the family left so suddenly from Washington, I couldn't deal with the excruciating pain of losing these kind souls I had only known for a short while.

Tonight, as I look at all of us together in this stadium, I realize we were meant to be together. Every one of us is like a puzzle piece meant to interconnect, love, shape, and mold each other. Rae, Carissa, Katherine, and Kaden—all of them are part of me, connected through my dad.

My life was formed by the choices of others. When I met my new Aldana family, I felt a surge of warmth and unconditional love, a connection. I wanted to become part of their story forever.

Suddenly, I feel blessed to be standing in awe of something so good. They are my family, my true family.

CHAPTER 58 – Sophia

As I peer across the yard filled with party guests, I see my dear husband. The look on his face is one of peace and happiness. It is the face of the man I knew long ago—before Sarah. Now, he has reemerged, despite tragedy and heartbreak, as a better soul, a man with deeper love, able to embrace us all. My children now see their father in a more human light, filled with flaws, but also with faith. They embrace him more now than ever before, simply because he is their father.

My view of the world is different now. I am more open and loving than I was before Sarah came into our lives. What I've learned more than anything is that life can change in an instant.

In one moment, my husband gained an unknown daughter. In another moment, I became a stepmother to a complete stranger. My daughters and son gained a new sister. And in an earlier moment, Sarah discovered she wasn't the daughter of her own father, but instead was connected to someone completely outside of her world. All of these disconnected and separate pieces have now become part of a whole—a new family.

As all of these long lost pieces come together, this family, our new family, is bound by a strong spirit, love. Love, the great and unchanging force, unseen and untouched, now keeps us close, warm, and forgiving in times when our lives feel like they're falling apart.

It is said love is the greatest gift. After all the events in our lives, I believe this is true. But, most of all, love and family are two gifts made stronger together, making us fit perfectly together. Always connected.

AFTERWORD

In writing this novel, it was not my intention to bring harm to those involved in the events which inspired this story.

Since the novel is told from multiple perspectives, the thoughts and words of these characters are fabricated based on how they might have felt.

My children read and approved the novel when it was finished, as did my husband. As a Roman Catholic Christian, I believe God brings people and situations into our lives for a purpose. God's grace urged us to act in accordance to His will and not our own. Although painful emotions like those described in the book are difficult to overcome, we are restored to the people we were meant to be through God's love. We are meant to love and give love regardless of our circumstances. In doing so, I believe we become our better selves, more understanding, and connected to others around us.

I hope this story will inspire others living with similar revelations to extend open arms to those who are innocent, including the children unknown to their fathers. The blessings we have received in loving our own "Sarah" have multiplied and have brought joy we may never have known.

When others heard our story, many wept. We have been told they were in awe of the ways in which we chose to love.

God is great in His quiet ways, and those who listen can find unexpected blessings. I hope other children who have never known their birth parents will find them and be accepted with love. Nothing can replace lost time, but joy can be found in building memories yet to come. Love is the great motivator that stirs us to act to change what once was wrong into something so right. God bless you.

ABOUT THE AUTHOR

Genevieve Galvan Frenes spent her early years on the outskirts of Caruthers and then later, moved to Selma, California. She graduated from Selma High School in 1987.

She attended Fresno Pacific College (now University) and graduated in 1991 with Magna Cum Laude Honors. She received a Bachelor's Degree in Single Subject Teaching in English. In 2004, she completed her Master's Degree in Educational Administration at California State University, Fresno, with Phi Kappa Phi Society Honors. She has taught English at Hanford High School for 19 years.

Presently, she is married to her husband of twenty-four years, David. Together, they have five children. She resides in Hanford, California. This is the author's first novel.

24626274R00115

Made in the USA
San Bernardino, CA
30 September 2015